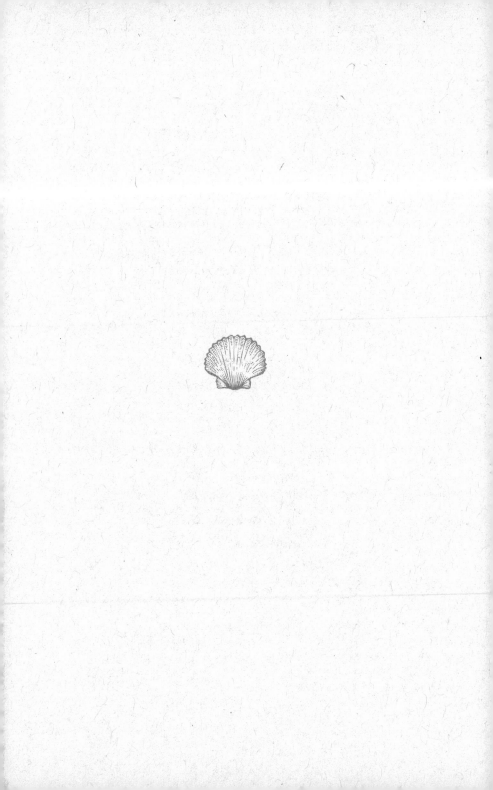

MYSTERIES *of* MARTHA'S VINEYARD

MYSTERIES *of* MARTHA'S VINEYARD

Seascape in Shadows

NANCY MEHL

Guideposts

New York

Mysteries of Martha's Vineyard is a trademark of Guideposts.

Published by Guideposts Books & Inspirational Media
110 William Street
New York, NY 10038
Guideposts.org

Cover and interior design by Müllerhaus
Cover illustration by Greg Copeland, represented by Deborah Wolfe, LTD.
Typeset by Aptara, Inc.

Printed and bound in the United States of America
10 9 8 7 6 5 4 3 2 1

CHAPTER ONE

Priscilla had just poured her second cup of coffee when the phone rang. The caller ID showed that the call was coming from the Art Attack, an art store in Tisbury. She frowned at the phone. She'd dropped off a painting to be cleaned yesterday afternoon. Surely they couldn't be done already.

"Hello?" she said.

"Priscilla, this is Roxie Darby at the Art Attack. I need to talk to you about your painting. Can you come by sometime today?"

"Is everything all right?" Priscilla asked. The painting, which had hung over her fireplace for many years, was precious to her. Had they done something to damage it?

"The painting is fine, it's just that . . . Well, I'd rather talk to you in person if you don't mind."

A small frisson of concern shot through Priscilla. She took a deep breath and let it out slowly. No sense in getting upset until she knew what was going on. "It might be this afternoon before I can get there. Is that okay?"

"That's fine. We're getting ready for this year's festival, so I'll be here all day."

"Okay, Roxie. I'll see you later today."

Priscilla hung up the phone. She'd taken the painting to Roxie because years of neglect had left the canvas darkened and dirty. Her aunt Marjorie, who'd left her cottage on Martha's Vineyard to Priscilla, had never seen to its condition. Priscilla loved the painting that portrayed her cozy cottage next to the lighthouse. Hopefully, trying to restore its original beauty wouldn't end up ruining it. Roxie was the new owner of the Art Attack. The previous owner, Aleeta Armbruster, had become embroiled in a scandal that involved selling fake paintings. Although she hadn't gone to jail over it, she'd eventually sold her shop and moved away.

Jake whined from behind Priscilla. She turned to find him with his leash in his mouth. The look on his face made her laugh. "Yes, I know. I haven't forgotten you. We go out every morning. Bringing me your leash really isn't necessary."

Jake opened his mouth in a doggy smile, dropping the leash on the floor. His deep brown eyes sparkled. Priscilla got up from her chair and rubbed his head. "Let me get my coat, and we'll go out now."

Once she was bundled up and Jake was wearing his leash instead of carrying it, the two stepped outside. It was the beginning of October, but it felt more like December. Fall temperatures had plummeted, and the citizens of Tisbury were worried that the weather might affect their Fall for the Arts Festival. Every year, visitors poured into Martha's Vineyard to visit shops and galleries full of local art and crafts. Last year, Priscilla's cousin Joan had shown four of her paintings, but this year she'd decided not to get involved in the festival.

Jake and Priscilla walked past the beautiful lighthouse and headed toward the cliff wall. Priscilla loved the sound of the waves hitting the shore. After living most of her life in Kansas, the incredible ocean scenery right outside her door still thrilled her.

She and Jake walked along the edge of the cliff, stopping once in a while for Jake to do his business. However, most of his time was spent sniffing out new smells and looking for sea gulls. He loved to bark at them. Most of them had gotten used to him and now purposely ignored him. Of course, that just made him bark even more. However, this morning the seagulls seemed to be congregating somewhere else.

After about fifteen minutes, Priscilla's face felt frozen solid. "Come on, Jake. Have mercy on me. I don't have a long furry coat like you do." She tugged on his leash and he reluctantly obeyed, walking next to her as they turned back toward the cottage.

As they ambled home, a car pulled up and parked next to the house and a man got out. He saw Priscilla and Jake coming his way and waited for them.

"Can I help you?" Priscilla asked when they got close enough for him to hear. He was middle-aged with thick brown hair and a goatee.

"I'm sorry to bother you," the man said, "but I wondered if it would be all right for me to sketch your lighthouse."

"Of course," Priscilla said with a smile. "Thanks for asking. A lot of people don't."

"I assume you have quite a few would-be artists showing up to draw this lovely landscape," he said.

"Yes, I do. I'm glad it inspires people with artistic talent."

The man laughed. "Not sure that applies to me, but I'd love to give it a try."

"All I ask is that you don't leave trash behind," she said. "I hope your efforts turn out well."

"Me too." The man stuck his hand out. "I'm Tucker Samuels."

Priscilla took his hand while Jake sat watching their exchange. He didn't seem too concerned about Tucker. "Priscilla Grant. Nice to meet you. You picked a cold day to sketch."

Tucker shrugged. "I'll only be in town a short time. I'm afraid I'll have to brave the chilly temperatures." He smiled at her. "I'll get out of your hair now. Thanks again for your hospitality."

Priscilla smiled again at him as he got back into his car and drove over near the lighthouse. She had gotten used to people coming by, wanting to draw or paint the lighthouse. It was beautiful, as was the coastline it watched over.

When Priscilla got inside, she decided to call Joan and see if she wanted to meet for lunch. Joan worked mornings at a local hospital as an ultrasound technician. Although Priscilla loved all three of her cousins, she was closest to Joan. Also a widow, she seemed to understand Priscilla more than her sister, Trudy, and their cousin Gail.

As Priscilla hung up her coat, she was grateful to be inside her warm house. Even Jake seemed happy to be back. He wasn't too keen on cold or rain. Warm summer walks were his favorite.

Priscilla called Joan to see about lunch, and they agreed to meet at the Little House Cafe where Priscilla promised she'd tell Joan all about Roxie's call. After she got off the phone, Priscilla spent the rest of the morning cleaning the house. A recent spill in the oven had caused a mess that she didn't want to harden into something akin to concrete, so she put on rubber gloves, got out the cleaner, and scrubbed for a while to make the inside of her oven sparkle. When she was finished, she realized it was almost eleven. She quickly pulled off her gloves, took a quick shower, and finished getting ready before jumping into her car and driving to nearby Tisbury.

She pulled into the parking lot right on time. Joan's car was already there so Priscilla hurried inside. She spotted her cousin sitting at a table in the corner and made her way over to where Joan waited.

"Thanks for agreeing to meet me for lunch," Priscilla said when she reached the table. "We haven't had much time to chat lately."

Joan smiled. "I talked to you at church two days ago."

Priscilla sat down in the chair next to Joan. "I know, but that was just small talk. We haven't had a real heart-to-heart for a while."

"You're right. Sorry. Like I told you, I've been working extra hours. Some of our staff have been out with the flu. I'm glad I didn't get it. Things are back to normal now, so I'm taking some time off this week."

"I'm glad." Priscilla smiled at her cousin. Joan was a no-nonsense person. Small, quick, and smart, she was someone Priscilla relied on to tell her the truth, not just what she wanted to hear. She appreciated that quality in people. Honesty was important to Priscilla, and Joan was extremely straightforward. Maybe a little too much sometimes.

"So how's Sister?" Priscilla asked.

Sister was a birthday gift from Priscilla, a tan-and-white blue heeler she had rescued from the local shelter. Joan had lost her dog Champ a few months before Priscilla moved to Martha's Vineyard, and Sister had been Priscilla's attempt to help fill the void he left. Sister had been a bit of a challenge at first, but she was doing well now.

Joan's eyes grew shiny. "I love her to pieces, Priscilla. I don't know what I'd do without her. My house had grown too quiet. Now there's always someone there. Someone who loves me and accepts me no matter what dumb thing I do."

"I don't think you do *dumb* things, and I expect Sister feels fortunate to have you in her life too."

"I hope so. Now, let's order. Then I want you to tell me about Roxie's call."

Before Priscilla could respond, their waitress came to the table. Priscilla asked for a steak sandwich and sweet potato fries. The small restaurant made the best steak sandwich she had ever tasted. Grilled sirloin on ciabatta bread with lettuce, tomato, and herbed feta cheese. Joan ordered the broiled chicken salad sandwich with grapes, crisp apples, and walnuts on a croissant.

"There's not much to say," Priscilla said. "Roxie wouldn't tell me why she wants to talk to me."

"That's odd," Joan said.

Priscilla nodded. "I'm a bit worried. I would hate to see one of Aunt Marjorie's paintings ruined."

Joan frowned at her. "Where did you get the idea that Aunt Marjorie painted it?"

"I...I don't know. I guess I assumed..."

"She didn't. In fact, it's a bit of a mystery."

"What do you mean?"

"When I was a girl, I asked her about the painting. She laughed and said, 'That was a gift from a secret admirer, honey. I guess I had a boyfriend who was too shy to reveal himself.'"

Priscilla's mouth dropped open. "Aunt Marjorie had a secret admirer?"

"Don't look so shocked," Joan said. "Marjorie was young once, you know. And she was attractive."

Priscilla giggled. "Okay, if you say so. I guess I always think of her as old Aunt Marjorie." She sighed. "At least I feel a little better. I still love that painting, but if something has happened to it, I won't beat myself up as much, knowing she didn't paint it."

When the waitress brought their food, the conversation turned to recent family events. Thankfully, everyone was doing well except for Gail's father, Hugh, who had come down with a nasty case of the flu. Gail lived with her father, who was dealing with some of the issues that come with age.

"He seems to have finally turned the corner," Joan said. "Poor Gail has certainly had her hands full."

"I'm glad to hear he's doing better," Priscilla said. Uncle Hugh was a dear man, greatly loved by his family as well as Jake. Jake and Uncle Hugh were crazy about each other.

When Priscilla and Joan finished their lunch, they left for the Art Attack. Even though it was cold outside, they walked since it wasn't far. Priscilla loved to stroll down the wooden walkways in Tisbury, looking into the windows of the wonderful little shops. When they entered the Art Attack, there were several people waiting to talk to Roxie. It was easy to tell they were hopeful artists who wanted their creations included in the festival. From what Priscilla could see, most of their work didn't hold a candle to Joan's paintings.

When Roxie saw them, she waved them over. "Excuse me for a moment," she told the woman trying to get her to showcase some embroidered pillowcases. "I'll be right back." She pointed toward the shop's back room. Priscilla and Joan followed Roxie past stacks of art supplies until they found themselves standing next to an older gentleman who had Priscilla's painting up on an easel.

"Priscilla and Joan, this is Charles Whistler. I hired him to clean your painting since he's very experienced in restoring and reviving older art pieces. I'm going to let him explain to you what he found."

"Nice to meet you, Charles," Priscilla said.

"And you too," the man said.

Priscilla guessed him to be in his late seventies or early eighties. He had a thick shock of white hair, bushy white eyebrows, and deep blue eyes that displayed intelligence. Lines around his eyes made it clear he smiled a lot, even if he wasn't smiling now.

"If you'll step closer," Charles said, "I want to show you something." He pointed to the right bottom corner of the painting.

"I was concerned about that," Priscilla said. "It looked as if some of the paint had flaked off there. I was hoping to have that fixed."

"I think that might be a mistake," Charles said. "When I looked closer I saw something exciting. I hope you won't be angry, but I scraped off a little more paint."

"I don't understand," Priscilla said. "Why would you do that?"

"Because of what I read. If you look carefully, you'll see a signature. There is another painting under this one."

"Really? Why would anyone paint over another painting?"

"It's done more than you might think," Roxie said. "For all kinds of reasons. Usually, it's because an artist is trying to save money on canvasses. But this is different."

Priscilla shook her head. "I don't understand," she said again.

"The signature," Charles said. "It's Arthur Melton Adair."

Joan gasped and Priscilla turned to look at her.

"Does that mean something to you?" she asked her cousin.

"Mrs. Grant," Charles said. "Arthur Melton Adair is an extremely famous New England artist. If the painting under yours is his . . . Well, it would be worth a great deal of money. You'll be a very wealthy woman."

CHAPTER TWO

After giving Roxie permission to remove the top painting, Priscilla and Joan left the shop. Priscilla stood on the sidewalk, trying to digest the information she'd received from Charles Whistler.

"I can't believe it," Joan said. "Why would someone paint over something done by Arthur Melton Adair? I doubt Adair painted your cottage and your lighthouse. It certainly wasn't his style."

"Well now at least I know it wasn't Aunt Marjorie," Priscilla said. "Even though she was a talented painter."

"So now what?" Joan asked. She pulled her coat collar up in an attempt to protect herself against the bone-chilling wind. Priscilla found herself shivering.

"Now we go somewhere warm. How about Candy's?" Candy Lane Confectionery, a local bakery, had great baked goods and all kinds of flavored coffee. At that moment, hot coffee sounded wonderful.

Joan nodded. "Sounds good. You lead, and I'll follow."

Since it was too far to walk, especially in the cold, the women got into their cars and drove to the popular bakery. Once inside, they went to the counter. Joan ordered a cream puff, and Priscilla asked for a slice of orange-cranberry bread. Both women ordered pumpkin spice lattes.

Once they had their food and coffee, Priscilla and Joan headed toward one of the café-style tables on one side of the restaurant. Before they got too far, they ran into Candy, who was talking to a couple sitting at a nearby table.

"Hello, ladies," Candy said with a wide smile. Her apron had a light dusting of flour, evidence that she'd been baking. "I see you ordered pumpkin spice lattes. Aren't they yummy?"

Priscilla nodded. "So good, they should be available all year, don't you think?"

Candy laughed. This wasn't the first time Priscilla had challenged Candy's decision to make the delicious drinks available only through October until the end of the year.

"I agree," Joan interjected. "They're so popular, Candy. You'd sell lots of them if you kept them on the menu."

Candy tossed her head and winked. "But if they become commonplace, my customers won't go out of their way to order them. As it is now, I sell so many before the end of the year, I don't need to make them a permanent menu item."

Priscilla sighed. "I understand, but we're going to keep trying, you know."

Candy grinned. "I wouldn't expect less. Enjoy, my friends."

With that, she swept past them, probably on her way to create a new baked good that would end up making Priscilla's jeans a little harder to button.

Joan and Priscilla found an empty table and sat down. "You must be really excited about the painting," Joan said after taking a bite of her cream puff. "I wonder how much it's worth?"

"Maybe we shouldn't get ahead of ourselves," Priscilla said. "I hate losing the original painting. I'm so fond of it. What if this Charles person is wrong?"

"He seemed to know what he was talking about. And Roxie is pretty knowledgeable. I would have made the same choice you did."

"Telling me Marjorie didn't paint it helped. If it had been hers..."

"She would have told you to uncover the Adair and sell it." Joan laughed. "Aunt Marjorie was nothing if not pragmatic. She left her property to you because she wanted to bless you. If the painting is what they say it is, she'd want you to use it to your advantage."

"I guess so." A thought suddenly occurred to Priscilla. "I know what would lessen my disappointment. One of your paintings over the fireplace. You could paint the cottage and the lighthouse."

Joan put her coffee down, and her smile slipped. "I don't know, Priscilla. I paint flowers. I've never tried a landscape, let alone actual buildings. I'm not sure I could do it."

"Well, I believe you can. You're really talented, you know. The paintings you showed at the festival last year were a hit. You even had people who wanted to buy them."

"I know, but what you're asking might be beyond my ability."

"Would you at least try? I'd much rather have your work hanging over the mantel than something painted by a stranger."

Joan ran her hand through her short brown hair. "All right, I'll give it a try, but don't blame me if it's awful."

Priscilla leaned over and placed her hand on top of Joan's. "It will be beautiful. I'm sure of it."

They were quiet for a few minutes as they ate their desserts and sipped their coffee. Finally Priscilla said, "I still can't wrap my head around the reason someone would paint over the work of a famous artist. And what in the world was it doing in the cottage? Did Aunt Marjorie know about it?"

Joan shrugged. "If she did, she never mentioned it. I took her comment about the secret admirer as a joke. But maybe she was telling the truth. She liked Billy Manders. Maybe he painted it."

"The man she and my mother argued over?"

Joan nodded. "If he was an artist, I never heard about it." She was quiet for a moment. "Maybe whoever painted over it didn't know it was an Adair."

"But someone who was into art should have known what it was, right? And if he did know, why would he give it to Aunt Marjorie?" Priscilla shook her head. "That painting was over the mantel when I was eight years old. I know it was there the last summer we spent here. Before Mom and Aunt Marjorie had their falling-out."

"I remember, that's when she got it," Joan said. "She hung it over the mantel during your last summer visit. Maybe you don't remember that, but I do. She replaced one of her own paintings with it. That's when I asked her if she painted it, and she told me it was a gift from a secret admirer."

As Priscilla ate her last bite of orange-cranberry bread, she turned the situation over in her mind. Aunt Marjorie accepted a painting from someone. Someone who must have known it was hiding an Adair. "I'm sure Aunt Marjorie had no idea an Adair was under her painting," Priscilla said.

"I agree," Joan said immediately. "Marjorie would have been horrified if she'd known."

"Would it have been an expensive painting fifty years ago?" Priscilla asked Joan.

"Absolutely. Adair was already famous by then. I think he died in the thirties. I remember back then one of his paintings selling for over two hundred thousand dollars. Now? Some of his works have sold for over a million." Joan paused for a moment. It was clear that Joan was as confused and intrigued as Priscilla. "Maybe someone was hiding the Adair and planned to come back for it."

"If that were true, why did it stay where it was for so many years?"

Joan held her hands up as if surrendering. "This might be one mystery you never solve. We can't talk to Aunt Marjorie, and we have no clue where the painting came from."

"Maybe we need to find out who her secret admirer was. He might be the only person who can tell us the truth."

"Maybe…" Joan said, drawing the word out. She frowned at Priscilla. "I'm not sure we could find him after all this time."

"You might be right." Priscilla hated thinking she might never find out how the painting found its way to Marjorie's house—and who painted over it. Her curiosity had been engaged. Not being able to solve a puzzle—any puzzle—didn't sit well with her.

"So has Trudy approached you about helping with her church's Halloween party again this year?" Joan asked.

It was clear to Priscilla that Joan was trying to change the subject. "She mentioned it. I'd already planned to help. I think everyone enjoyed it last year."

"I do too. It was a great idea."

"At least this year we're prepared. The church still has the booths from last year. As long as we get enough volunteers, I think it will be even better this time."

"I'd be happy to help," Joan said. "I don't really have—"

She stopped talking when someone came up and stood next to their table. Priscilla looked up to see Gerald O'Bannon. Gerald was dressed in his uniform. As the captain of the Coast Guard station, he almost always wore his uniform during the day. He smiled at Priscilla, his hazel eyes looking deeply into hers. Priscilla felt something like a jolt of electricity run through her. He was so handsome. She tried to swallow past the lump she felt in her throat. "Hi, Gerald," she said, her voice squeakier than she wanted it to be.

"Hello yourself," he said back. "Good to see you."

"I forgot that you eat lunch here on Tuesdays."

Gerald smiled. "I've finished lunch. Just getting a pumpkin spice latte to go."

"But you're a black coffee drinker," Priscilla said.

"I've decided I need to shake things up a bit," Gerald said. "Seems I'm way too predictable."

"I didn't mean to imply anything like that." Priscilla was a little embarrassed. "You're just...a creature of habit."

"I guess that's true. Still, I like Candy's pumpkin coffee. I come by a couple of times a week to get a cup." He looked down at the table and chuckled. "I see you two feel the same way."

Priscilla nodded. "Nothing like Candy's special coffee on a cold day."

"So are you on your way back to the station?" Joan asked.

"Pretty soon. Just had lunch with Aggie. She left a few minutes ago." He shook his head. "She had some news that has really left me wondering what to do."

"Is it something you can talk about?" Priscilla asked. Aggie was Gerald's daughter. He was very close to her.

Gerald nodded. "Nick may be offered a great job in Boston. He's thinking about taking it. If he does, they'll all move after the first of the year. They want me to retire and move to be closer to them. I know we've been through this before, Priscilla. I wouldn't even consider it but I hate losing contact with them. I wouldn't get to see them very often."

Priscilla felt her stomach turn over. Just a month ago Gerald had been offered a promotion but had turned it down and decided to stay on the island. She thought this had been settled once and for all. How could this happen again? "So when would you go?" she asked, her voice still higher than normal.

Gerald held his hand up. "Whoa. I didn't say I'd go for sure. Nick hasn't gotten the official offer yet. Once he does, then I'll have to make a decision." He sighed. "The idea of being so far from Aggie and the kids...Well, it certainly isn't what I want."

Priscilla nodded. "I understand. I hope you'll let me know if you decide to go. We should have a going away party for you."

"That sounds great," Joan said, clapping her hands. "Something really special."

Gerald chuckled. "Before you start planning my departure, let's wait until we know for sure. Maybe they won't offer enough money and benefits. If they don't, Nick will turn them down."

Priscilla smiled and nodded, trying not to show how upset she really was. The sour feeling in her stomach had moved up to her throat, and she felt an overwhelming urge to get out of the restaurant. She needed fresh air. "Are you about ready?" she asked Joan.

Joan quickly drained the rest of her cup. "Yeah, I need to get going. I have some things to do this afternoon."

"Good to see you ladies," Gerald said. "Priscilla, can I call you later? Maybe dinner one night this week?"

"Uh, maybe," Priscilla said. "I've got a really busy week. We'll have to see."

She grabbed her purse and stood up. Joan did the same. "See you later," she said to Gerald. She walked quickly toward the front door, Joan struggling to keep up with her. When Priscilla got outside she stopped on the sidewalk and gulped in the cold air, trying to steady her jangled nerves.

Joan put her hand on Priscilla's arm. "He didn't say he was definitely leaving. Maybe Nick won't take the job."

Priscilla shrugged. "Doesn't matter to me what he does."

Joan sighed. "Priscilla..."

"Let's not talk about it." Priscilla turned and hugged Joan. "I've got to go. Talk to you soon." With that she hurried to her car, got inside, and started to drive away. When she looked in her rear-view mirror, she realized Joan was still standing on the sidewalk, watching her, a look of concern on her face. The sick feeling she'd felt earlier returned, and her stomach churned.

CHAPTER THREE

By the time Priscilla got back to the cottage, it was already three o'clock. She checked to see if Tucker was still on the property, but his car was gone. Probably couldn't take the cold. She was still heartsick about Gerald. She didn't want him to leave, but she certainly couldn't ask him to stay. Even though her husband, Gary, had been gone almost two years, Priscilla still found it hard to imagine sharing her life with anyone else. Still, she really liked Gerald. If there was anyone she could see herself having a future with, it was him. He'd said and done several things that led her to believe he had feelings for her too. If he was willing to move to Boston, did it mean he didn't care for her enough to stay in Martha's Vineyard? Or did it simply mean he wanted to be near his daughter and her family? She knew in her heart that it was the latter, but a twinge of insecurity wriggled around in her mind. Realizing that worrying about what Gerald might be thinking wasn't getting her anywhere, Priscilla forced herself to focus on something else.

She found herself staring up at the blank space over her fireplace. She hated losing the painting she'd grown used to seeing, even if Aunt Marjorie hadn't painted it.

Although the cottage was comfortable, Priscilla decided to start a fire. There was nothing more calming than a crackling fire and a cup of tea. She had just brewed a cup of peppermint tea when her doorbell rang. She wasn't expecting anyone and was surprised to find her cousin Trudy standing on her front porch. Priscilla ushered Trudy inside and out of the cold. Jake joined them, his tail wagging. Trudy was one of his favorite people. She reached down and stroked his soft face.

"Jakey, how are you?" Trudy twisted her neck so she could see Priscilla. "Sorry I didn't call. I wasn't far from here and decided to swing by. Are you busy?"

"No," Priscilla said with a smile. "I'd just brewed a cup of peppermint tea. Would you like some?"

"Sounds wonderful. Boy, is it cold out there."

Trudy pulled a knit cap off her head and slipped off her coat. Priscilla took them and hung them up.

"My hair's a mess," Trudy said. She reached up and tried to fluff out her curly blonde hair.

Priscilla laughed. "If I wore a hat like that, my hair would be flattened. Yours looks like you just left the hairdresser's."

"I'm sure you're being kind, but thanks. I got so irritated with it this morning, I just pulled that cap on and decided to ignore it altogether."

Although some women might make comments about their looks hoping to encourage others to soothe their egos, Trudy wasn't like that. Her blue eyes sparkled as she poked fun at herself.

She followed Priscilla through the living room and into the kitchen where she sat down at Priscilla's small breakfast table. Jake trotted behind them and curled up at Trudy's feet.

"So is this just a social visit?" Priscilla asked.

Trudy winked at her. "Yes and no." She cleared her throat, a warning to Priscilla that she was getting ready to ask for something. Priscilla had a pretty good idea what it was.

"Is this about Halloween?"

Trudy grinned. "You read my mind. Will you help us again this year? I promise it will be much, much easier. It was such a hit last year."

Priscilla poured boiling water over a teabag and took it to Trudy. "Actually, I'd love to be involved again. For the most part, it was a lot of fun."

Trudy giggled. "I think I can promise you we won't have all the drama of last year."

The year before someone had stolen money and jewelry from purses stored in the church's kitchen while volunteers worked in the gym. Thankfully, the thief was caught and everything was returned.

"I'm counting on that."

Priscilla sat down at the table next to Trudy. "Have you talked to Joan today?" she asked.

Trudy shook her head. "Why? What's up?"

Priscilla filled her in on the painting and everything that had taken place at the Art Attack. As she talked, Trudy's eyes grew larger and larger.

"Are you kidding?" she asked when Priscilla finished. "Wow. I wonder how much the painting is worth." She paused for a moment, a frown marring her pretty face. "I always assumed Aunt Marjorie painted that picture. If she didn't, who did?"

"I have absolutely no idea. Joan told me Aunt Marjorie mentioned a secret admirer, but that's not much to go on."

"No, it isn't," Trudy said. "You know, now that I think about it, I believe Joan told me once that Aunt Marjorie didn't paint that picture. I'd forgotten all about it." She shrugged. "Maybe it doesn't really matter. I mean, as long as the painting underneath is recovered." She took a sip of her tea. "I hope this guy at the Art Attack knows what he's doing. I mean, isn't removing paint from a canvas without harming the picture underneath rather difficult? I would imagine it takes a lot of experience."

"You're right," Priscilla said. "Roxie seems to think he can handle it. I don't really know this guy. She just hired him to clean the painting."

"What's his name?"

Priscilla thought a moment. What was it? "Charles…Whistler," she said, smiling. "I only remember his last name because of the artist James McNeill Whistler."

Trudy grinned. "The guy who painted *Whistler's Mother*, right?"

Priscilla smiled. "Yes, along with a lot of other things."

"I may not know much about artists, but I know Charles Whistler. He's lived on the island all his life. He was friends with Aunt Marjorie." Trudy looked off into the distance for a moment, obviously thinking. "I'm trying to remember…I think he used to paint. Aunt Marjorie said something about it once." She shook her head. "It was a long time ago. I just can't recall exactly what she said. Maybe Mildred knows him. I think they all used to be friends."

Mildred Pearson was the caretaker of the East Shore Historical Museum. Although she had a tough exterior, Priscilla had grown to appreciate her knowledge and her commitment to the island and the people who lived there—past and present.

"None of this makes much sense, does it?" Trudy said.

"No, but like I said, I thought the painting was something Aunt Marjorie did. She was a talented painter."

"Yes, she was."

There were several other paintings by Marjorie on the walls of the cottage. Most were seascapes.

"I can't see her painting over something by Arthur Melton Adair anyway. According to Joan, she would have known his work." Priscilla shrugged. "I had no idea who he was, but Joan knew immediately."

"Yeah, she would." Trudy took a sip of tea. "So now what?"

"Well, I'll wait until Charles finishes his work. Then we'll see what we have. If it's really valuable..." She looked at Trudy and shook her head. "I have no idea what to do. Does it belong to Aunt Marjorie? Do I keep an expensive painting here? Or do I give it to a museum?"

"Or do you sell it and make a lot of money?" Trudy said, grinning. "That's what I'd do."

"Somehow that doesn't feel right," Priscilla said slowly. "If only I knew how it ended up here."

"I certainly can't help you with that." Trudy downed the rest of her tea. "I'd better get going. Dan wants to go out for dinner tonight. I need to get ready."

Priscilla's eyebrows shot up. "How long does it take you? I can get ready in fifteen minutes."

Trudy giggled. "I'm much more vain than you are, dear cousin. By the time I pick out an outfit, do my makeup, and fix my hair, Dan will be waiting impatiently for me to 'Hurry up for Pete's sake.'"

Priscilla laughed. That sounded exactly like Dan. "I'll walk you to the door." She paused a moment and looked at the clock. "Maybe I'll hop over to the museum and talk to Mildred. If she could shed some light on the painting..."

Priscilla was interrupted by a knock on the door. Trudy followed her as she opened the door and found two police officers standing on her front porch.

And they didn't look happy.

CHAPTER FOUR

Hi, Hank," Trudy said to Tisbury's police chief. Hank Westin
and Trudy were old friends. They'd grown up together. He
was a large man, an imposing figure. At that moment, the expression on his face made him look a little intimidating. Officer Teddy
Holmes stood next to the chief, and the look on his face was as
sour as his boss's.

"Hi, Trudy," the chief said. He turned to Priscilla. "We need to
talk to you."

"Is something wrong?" she asked. Priscilla was running
through a list of friends and family members. Was everyone all
right? Was someone hurt?

"It's about the painting you took to the Art Attack," Teddy
said.

Priscilla heaved a sigh of relief. Everyone was safe. She pulled
the door open. "Please, come in. It's freezing out there."

Chief Westin and Teddy stepped inside the cottage, and
Priscilla waved toward the living room. "Sit down." Jake, who was
lying in front of the fireplace, lifted his head to stare at the two
men. He didn't seem to think they represented any kind of threat,
so he promptly went back to sleep.

"No, thank you," the chief said, removing his hat.

"What's going on, Hank?" Trudy asked. "You're acting as if Priscilla has committed a crime."

The chief cleared his throat, and Teddy looked decidedly uncomfortable. "I'm not saying she has," he said. "But someone has, and we need to get to the bottom of it as soon as we can."

"Look," Priscilla said, "I know there's a painting by a famous artist under the picture that's hung over the mantle in this house for...Well, for as long as I can remember. But how is that a crime?"

Hank stared at her. "It's a crime when it's a stolen painting."

Priscilla's mouth dropped open. "A—a what?"

"That's right. It was stolen fifty years ago from a traveling exhibit in Plymouth. It belongs to a museum in New York City. It's called *Seascape in Shadows* by Arthur Melton Adair."

"Well, I hope you're not accusing Priscilla of taking it," Trudy said sharply. "She would have been a child. And she lived in Kansas!"

Chief Westin sighed. "Of course I don't think she took it. But we need to find out how it got here. Your aunt..."

"Now hold on," Trudy said. "Aunt Marjorie wasn't a thief. You can't accuse her of something when she can't defend herself."

"I'm not accusing anyone of anything yet."

"I don't understand something," Priscilla said. "Charles couldn't have worked on the painting very long. I just gave him permission to remove the top layer of paint a few hours ago."

"The entire painting hasn't been uncovered yet. It didn't take long for him to figure out what the painting was. Roxie had him stop working. She contacted the Museum of Fine Arts in Boston.

They insisted that someone with more experience than Mr. Whistler finish the restoration process."

"I can understand that," Priscilla said. "Chief, I'm just now finding out about the other painting, just like everyone else. Obviously, if I'd known it was stolen and I had anything to do with the theft, I wouldn't have asked Charles to uncover it."

"I realize that," the chief said. "Again, you're not under any suspicion. Yet, anyway."

"Yet?" Trudy asked. She put her hands on her hips and glared at Hank. "What do you mean *yet?*"

The chief rolled his eyes and sighed. "I mean, the FBI plans to take over the investigation. As I said, the painting was owned by a gallery in New York and was stolen in Massachusetts. The crime crossed state lines, which makes it a federal case. The Feds are on their way now. Once they arrive, they'll decide what to do next."

"So the FBI might suspect me of knowing the painting was stolen?" Priscilla asked.

"You should have left it over the mantel where it was," Trudy said under her breath.

Priscilla shook her head. "No, it should go back where it belongs. I'm glad it's being recovered, but I certainly would like to know how it ended up in Aunt Marjorie's house."

"We'd like to know that too," Chief Westin said, putting his hat back on. He nodded at Teddy. "We need to get going. I just wanted to make you aware of what was going on."

Priscilla stuck her hand out and the chief shook it. "Thanks, Chief. If there's anything I can do to help…"

"I'll let you know. But…" He turned a little pink and cleared his throat. "Please don't leave the island. The FBI will want to talk to you."

Priscilla didn't respond. She just nodded. *Don't leave the island?* It reminded her of the crime shows she'd watched where the police informed the suspect *not to leave town.*

After Hank and Teddy left, Priscilla turned to Trudy. "I can't believe this is happening."

Trudy frowned. "Neither can I. Aunt Marjorie wouldn't hide a stolen painting. I'm certain of that. But I have a feeling it's what people will think."

"We'll just have to prove her innocence."

Trudy smiled. "If anyone can do it, you can."

Priscilla returned her smile. "You mean *we* can."

"Uh-oh. That's my cue to leave." Trudy grabbed her coat, patted Jake on the head, and gave her cousin a big hug. "Keep me updated."

Priscilla hugged her back. "I will."

After Trudy left, Priscilla sat down and finished her tea. She pondered memories of the last time she visited the island before moving here last year. She was only eight years old. It was Thanksgiving, and Priscilla's mother and Aunt Marjorie had a terrible argument over Billy Manders. "So Joan said Marjorie hung the painting the last summer I was here," Priscilla said to Jake who watched her with interest. She thought for a moment. "Who was around here fifty years ago who might know who gave the painting to her?" Jake flashed her a doggy smile and put his head down again. "You're not much help, are you?" Priscilla said, smiling. She ran through several residents of nearby Tisbury in her mind and settled on Trudy's suggestion. Mildred knew more about the history of Martha's Vineyard—and Tisbury—than anyone else. Her expertise seemed to include a lot of personal knowledge as well as the kind of facts found in history books.

Priscilla checked the time. The museum was still open. If she hurried, she could talk to Mildred today. Priscilla's curiosity and her desire to protect her aunt drove her to head out into the cold again. She gave Jake a chance to go with her, but he turned his head away and ignored her invitation.

"Okay, big baby. I'll be back soon."

Priscilla hurried out to her car. With the threat of Gerald leaving and the revelations about the stolen painting, today was certainly shaping up to be interesting—as well as rather disturbing. Priscilla prayed both situations would resolve themselves in a positive way.

CHAPTER FIVE

When Priscilla arrived at the East Shore Historical Museum, it was quiet, with only a few visitors. She loved the museum, with its rooms decorated in different styles, including an 1812 parlor, an 1850s dining room and a 1790s pantry. Mildred liked to dress in historical garb and today she wore a long russet-colored skirt gathered at the waist, with a long-sleeved fitted waistcoat over a white bodice. A lace collar circled her neck, and lace cuffs adorned her wrists. Her gray hair was pulled tightly back and covered with a white coif.

When she spotted Priscilla, she gestured for her to come over.

"I love your outfit," Priscilla said. "Tell me about it."

Mildred gave her a small smile. "This is how the Pilgrims really dressed. All those pictures of black dresses with large white bibs? Although some wore clothing somewhat like that, most Pilgrims enjoyed different colors, and the women dressed more like this."

Priscilla chuckled. "I honestly didn't know that. Seems I learn something every time I talk to you, Mildred."

Mildred pointed to a table a few feet away. Although there were several people in the museum, it wasn't very busy. "How about a cup of coffee and one of Candy's cookies? I have some left over from the History Tea yesterday."

"That would be wonderful, thank you."

Priscilla took a seat while Mildred headed to the kitchen located in the back of the museum. She emerged a couple of minutes later with two cups of coffee and a plate of cookies.

"I take it this isn't a casual visit?" Mildred asked when she sat down at the table. "Does this have something to do with the stolen painting?"

Priscilla sighed. Tisbury didn't need regular media outlets to spread news. The citizens had their own way of sharing information at the speed of gossip.

"Don't be upset," Mildred said. "Finding a famous painting in Tisbury is a big deal."

"I understand, but once in a while it would be nice to keep something to myself." Priscilla took a sip of coffee. Rich and flavorful, it was exactly what she needed at the moment. She put her cup down and met Mildred's curious gaze. "Look, I know this is a long shot, but do you have any idea how my aunt acquired that painting? The only thing Joan could remember was that Marjorie said a secret admirer gave it to her. The rest of us thought Marjorie painted it."

Mildred's eyes widened. It was obvious her question hit a nerve. Priscilla leaned closer to her friend. "What can you tell me, Mildred? People may think Marjorie had something to do with the theft unless we can figure out who gave her that painting."

Mildred picked up her own coffee cup and took a slow sip. When she set it down, she sighed. "I don't know exactly who gave it to her, but I can narrow it down for you." She reached up to check her coif. Priscilla felt like she was stalling. Thinking. What was there to think about?

"Fifty years ago there was a small group of artists in Tisbury who studied together." Mildred's words were slow and deliberate. As if she was being careful to say the right thing. "The group included Marjorie, Tilly Synder, me, Billy Manders, Alma Whitaker, Charles Whistler, a couple of other people who have since moved away, and...your mother. We called ourselves the Tisbury Collective."

Priscilla's mouth dropped open. "But...Mom didn't live here fifty years ago."

"She was here when the group started. And after she got married and left the island, you all used to visit in the summers, which is when the group got together. I think the collective met for three summers before it shut down. The man who taught the class, Adrian Deering, was a teacher on the island. He could only lead us when school was out. Of course, after Charlotte and Marjorie fell out, your mother was never part of the group again. Not that it mattered. We stopped meeting not long after that summer ended."

Priscilla couldn't remember her mother mentioning an art class. Of course, when they visited the island, Priscilla spent most of her time playing with her cousins. She didn't pay that much attention to what her parents were doing. It was true that Mom wasn't around all the time, but why didn't she say something? Priscilla wondered if her father knew about the class. She assumed he did, but she couldn't remember him mentioning anything about it. "Do you have any idea how that painting ended up at my aunt's house, Mildred? Do you know who painted over it?"

Instead of answering, Mildred took another drink of coffee. When she put the cup down, she looked away for a moment. Then she said, "I really don't know anything concrete about the Adair painting—or who painted the cottage and the lighthouse and gave it to your aunt. All I can tell you is that things were very strange at that time. There were . . . secrets." She fixed her gaze on Priscilla. "I don't know everything that was going on, but it had something to do with Billy Manders. I believe there was more to the argument between your mother and your aunt than just a misunderstanding about their feelings for Billy."

"Is there someone else who might know more than you do about Billy Manders?"

Mildred paused for a moment. Priscilla could see the conflict on her face. "I can't be sure. He wasn't really close to anyone in the group. Except maybe Raymond. But by the end of that summer they weren't speaking for some reason." She sighed. "He occasionally talked to Tilly, but she was kind to everyone. We all got along with Tilly. Just because they talked some, it doesn't mean he shared his secrets with her." Mildred shook her head slowly. "Of course, we all heard about the theft of *Seascape in Shadows*. It was big news."

"I suppose trying to remember who might have been out of town when the painting was stolen would be impossible after all this time."

Mildred nodded. "Absolutely impossible. For me anyway." She waved her hand toward the books lining one wall of the museum. "I try to remind people about our history, but I need help from the people who wrote it down. Took note of it. Remembering who was where fifty years ago? I can't help you. All I can say is that nothing sticks out in my mind. Of course, as I said, I have no reason to believe anyone you know was involved."

"Including my aunt?"

Mildred chuckled. "Especially your aunt. Marjorie had great respect for art—and for right and wrong. She was a good Christian woman. There's no way in the world she would have stolen a painting—or hidden one. I will never believe that nor will anyone who knew her."

Priscilla sighed. "I hope you're right. My cousins and I feel as if we need to defend her reputation." She drained her cup. "The FBI is coming. I'm afraid they won't be so willing to accept the word of people who think Marjorie was an honest woman. They may want more proof than that."

"And what kind of proof can we give them?" Mildred asked, arching her back and frowning at Priscilla. "Marjorie isn't here to defend herself. I'm not sure they'll be willing to accept our assurances."

"You might be right. Of course, there isn't anything that would tie my aunt to this theft. But…"

"You don't want her name dragged through the mud."

Priscilla nodded. "The funny thing is, I feel guilty somehow. Just for having the painting. It's odd."

"Not that odd. Just keep reminding yourself that you had nothing to do with hanging that painting in your house."

Mildred's comment was said with compassion, not something Priscilla was used to hearing from her no-nonsense friend. "Thank you, Mildred. I will definitely try to remember that." Priscilla stood up. "And thank you for the coffee and cookies. I feel better."

"Candy's cookies can turn any day around."

Priscilla laughed. "I think you're right about that." She said goodbye and left. When she got into her car she ran her discussion with Mildred over in her mind. At least she had a starting point. But where would it lead her? Was it too late to find the truth after all these years?

CHAPTER SIX

When Priscilla returned to the cottage, her phone was ringing. She hurried to pick it up. It was Trudy.

"I've been calling your cell phone," she said right away, sounding a bit accusatory, "but it kept going to voice mail."

"Oh, Trudy. I'm sorry. I put it on silent while I was visiting Mildred. I completely forgot to turn it back on."

"You talked to Mildred? Did you learn anything?"

Priscilla briefly went over what Mildred had told her.

"Well, that's interesting," Trudy said. "Makes you wonder if the group had something to do with the disappearance of the painting. But finding out the truth after this many years might be tough."

"Exactly what I've been thinking," Priscilla said with a sigh.

"I called Joan and Gail. We need to get together and talk about what's going on. How about meeting us for dinner tonight?"

"I thought you and Dan were going out."

"Something came up at work and he had to go in." She laughed. "Not sure what kind of emergency a marine biologist can have, but it happens from time to time."

"I'm sorry your date didn't work out, but I think getting together is a great idea." A thought popped into Priscilla's mind.

"How about the Colonial Inn? It seems Tilly may know something about the painting. We could kill two birds with one stone."

"Sounds good to me. Seven o'clock?"

"Perfect. I'll see you all there." When she hung up, she felt better. Having her cousins involved in helping her search for the truth took some of the pressure off. They were smart, and they'd lived here much longer than she had. They were liable to have a better perspective. She wondered about the people in the Tisbury Collective. Marjorie, Tilly, Alma, Mildred, her mother, Billy Manders, Charles Whistler, and the teacher, Adrian Deering. Oh, and Raymond...what was his last name? Was it Hill? Priscilla couldn't help but wonder about Charles. He was in the collective—and he'd discovered the painting. A strange coincidence. Priscilla needed to find out more about him. Mildred had mentioned another person who'd moved away. Priscilla planned to follow up on everyone, even those who didn't live in Tisbury anymore. Although Mildred had been forthcoming, she still wanted to talk to Tilly. Of course, that was if she could pin her down for a bit. Tilly was a free spirit. She loved to glide around her restaurant and visit with her customers. Hopefully Priscilla could get her to settle down for a few minutes. She really wanted Tilly's perspective. She was an honest person, and Priscilla trusted her. She felt Tilly would be candid with her about the collective.

She spent the rest of the afternoon cleaning the kitchen. Since the oven was pristine, the rest of the kitchen felt dirty. After wiping down the insides of cabinets and putting things back, she finally stopped to freshen up and get ready to meet her cousins. Before leaving, she took Jake out again. He didn't take long to do his business, and quickly wanted back in where it was warm. "You're worse than me," she told him when he ran over and lay down in front of the fireplace. "Sorry, bud, but not while I'm gone. I'm afraid you'll have to sit in front of the vent if you want warmth." As if he understood her, he got up and went over to where an air vent in the wall pushed out warm air. Priscilla laughed. He'd discovered the vent a few days ago. When the fire wasn't lit, the vent was his second choice.

After grabbing her coat, gloves, scarf, and hat, Priscilla stepped outside. It seemed even colder now. Normally, it was in the sixties and seventies in October. No one was prepared for this strange cold snap. Although Priscilla loved winter, she had to admit that she wasn't ready for the cold to come this early.

Thankfully her SUV heated up quickly. The warm air felt great. When she pulled into the parking lot at the Colonial Inn, she was relieved to see it wasn't very busy. Most people seemed to go out to eat on the weekends, so tonight's crowd was usually light. That gave Priscilla a better chance to speak to Tilly. Priscilla parked and then went inside. She found Joan and Gail waiting just inside the entrance.

"So glad to see you," Gail said, hugging her. "Believe it or not, Trudy isn't here yet, but let's go ahead and get a table."

"She's never late," Priscilla said. "I think she loves arriving before we do. I hope everything's okay."

"I'm sure she'll have a good reason," Joan said, "but if she doesn't show up soon, I'll call her."

"Did she bring you up to date on my conversation with Mildred?"

Joan and Gail nodded at the same time.

"First time I've ever heard about the Tisbury Collective," Joan said. "It's interesting."

Before Priscilla could respond the hostess came to take them to their table. As they entered the dining room Priscilla looked around for the eccentric restaurant owner but didn't see her. When they sat down, Priscilla asked the hostess if Tilly was available.

She frowned. "I saw her earlier, but I'm not sure where she is now. If I see her would you like me to ask her to stop by your table?"

Priscilla smiled and shook her head. "No, that's okay. Thanks anyway."

"Why did you say that?" Joan asked as the hostess walked away. "I thought you wanted to talk to her."

"I do, but I don't want her to feel like I'm interrogating her. I want our conversation to seem more casual."

"So what's your plan?" Gail asked. "'Is the grilled tilapia good tonight? And by the way, do you know anything about a valuable stolen painting?'"

Priscilla grunted. "No, of course not." She stared at the menu in front of her. "Actually, I have no idea what I'm going to say. No matter how you frame it, it sounds like I'm suspicious about the Tisbury Collective."

"Here comes Trudy," Joan said.

Priscilla turned to see Trudy hurrying toward them, her blonde curls bouncing underneath a cute red beret that matched her red coat. Priscilla was amused by how different Trudy was from her other cousins. Joan and Gail looked and acted similar. They both had brown hair and were much more reserved. Most people would have guessed them to be sisters rather than cousins. Trudy, on the other hand was a true extrovert. Blonde hair, blue eyes, always in a hurry. Always the life of the party.

"Sorry to be late," she said as she plopped down into her chair.

"We were worried about you," Priscilla said. "You're never late for anything."

Trudy waved dismissively. "I have a very good reason. I saw Alma Whitaker coming out of the library, so I stopped and talked to her."

"Oh, Trudy," Priscilla said. "I hope you didn't bring up the collective. I want to be careful how we go about gathering information. If we make people feel like we suspect them, they might not tell us what we need to know."

Trudy slipped off her coat and put in on the back of her chair. "Give me a little credit, please. I'm not a total idiot."

"So what happened?" Gail said. "What did she say?"

"We didn't talk very long. It's so cold outside." Trudy leaned into the table. "I asked her if she'd heard about the painting found in the cottage. She said she had, but she acted really nervous. I made some comment about how odd it was—that we knew Aunt Marjorie would never be involved in hiding a valuable painting. She said, and I quote, 'You never know what people might do when they have no other choice.' Then she walked away."

Priscilla's mouth dropped open. "What in the world does that mean?"

Trudy straightened in her chair. "I have no idea, but it was certainly a strange thing to say." She picked up her fork and pointed it at her sister and her cousins. "She knows something, ladies. Something she clearly doesn't want to talk about."

"But why would she respond in a way that would obviously raise suspicions?" Joan asked. "It doesn't make sense. If I was involved somehow, I'd tell you I knew nothing about it. I certainly wouldn't make an odd comment like that."

"I agree," Priscilla said.

Hilda, one of the waitresses at the Inn, stepped up to the table. "Can I get you ladies something to drink?" she asked.

Hilda was a staple at the Inn. It was hard to guess how old she was, but Priscilla guessed her to be in her late fifties or early sixties. She wasn't the fastest waitress in town, but she was steady and reliable. And she knew the menu by heart. She also knew exactly how her customers liked their food and remembered everyone she served.

Her cousins asked for coffee, but Priscilla had already had too much and didn't want to face a sleepless night. She ordered a glass of water with lemon.

Hilda traipsed off for the kitchen while the women went back to their discussion.

"So what do we do now?" Joan asked. "We've talked to two of the people in the collective." She frowned at Priscilla. "Go through the list again for me?"

Priscilla took a small notepad out of her purse. "Mildred said the group included her, Aunt Marjorie, my mother, Billy Manders, Tilly Snyder, Alma Whitaker, and Charles Whistler. Oh, and the teacher, Adrian Deering."

"Didn't you say there were a couple of people who moved away?" Trudy asked.

"Yes, that's right. Raymond Hill...and someone else."

"We need to find out where they are," Gail said. "Wouldn't the guilty person leave town?"

"Not if they wanted to stay near the painting," Joan said. "But why let it sit there all these years? The thief could have retrieved it anytime."

"That is strange," Priscilla said.

"Maybe they were afraid to snatch it back," Trudy added. "They didn't want to get caught."

"But why paint over it at all?" Joan said. "I'm not an expert on art, but even I know painting over another painting could ruin the original work."

"You're right," Gail said thoughtfully. "Unless hiding it was more important than selling it."

The women were silent as they considered Gail's point. Was fear of getting caught more important than selling the painting and making a fortune?

As if reading Priscilla's mind, Joan said, "But you can't sell a painting like that. One so famous."

"You have to offer it on the black market," Trudy said, arching her eyebrows.

Joan laughed. "What do you know about the black market, Trudy?"

Trudy scowled at her sister. "More than you might think." She reached into her purse and pulled her phone out. "First of all, would you like to see *Seascape in Shadows*?"

"Absolutely." Priscilla couldn't believe it hadn't occurred to her to look it up. Concern about the painting and thinking about Gerald seemed to have taken up most of the space in her brain.

Trudy's red fingernails clicked on her phone's screen. Then she held it out. Priscilla caught her breath as she stared at the image on the screen. It was incredible. The artist had painted a stormy sea from the view of a New England cliff. Done in grays and blues, the clouds cast shadows over the water and the land. It was compelling and almost unearthly.

"Oh, I hope they can save it," she whispered. "It's beautiful." She passed the phone to Joan, who shared Priscilla's appreciation of the painting.

"If I had talent like this, I'd paint every day of my life," she said softly.

Gail shook her head when the phone was passed to her. "It's really something. Breathtaking."

Trudy had just reached for her phone when Hilda came back to the table with their drinks. "It's hard to believe someone could steal something so wonderful," Trudy said. "Something everyone should be able to enjoy."

Hilda glanced down at the phone and gasped. Her tray hit the floor with a loud crash.

CHAPTER SEVEN

The sound of shattering ceramic coffee cups echoed through the restaurant as customers froze in place. The look of horror on Hilda's face spurred Priscilla to action. She got up from her chair and took Hilda's arm.

"It's okay," she said. "Accidents happen. Let me help you clean this up." Priscilla knelt down and began to put the broken pieces on the tray that had landed next to the wreckage. From somewhere behind her, a loud voice rang out.

"Leave that alone. We'll take care of it."

Priscilla knew who it was but she continued to pick up some of the larger pieces. She felt bad for Hilda and didn't mind helping.

When Tilly reached them, she touched Priscilla's shoulder. "Thank you for helping, but we'll clean this up. It's not your responsibility."

Priscilla stood up and found herself looking into Tilly's face. Her large dark eyes bored into Priscilla's. Tilly, often called "Miss Tilly," was a petite dynamo. Although she was older than Priscilla, her face was unlined, making it hard to guess her age. There was an energy that emanated from Tilly Snyder. She was a force to be reckoned with. "It's not a problem," Priscilla said softly. "It was an accident."

Tilly's expression softened. "I appreciate that, Priscilla, but we can do it faster. And if you cut yourself, it would make things worse."

Priscilla could see that Hilda was embarrassed, and she didn't want to do anything to add to her discomfort. As she slipped back into her chair, another staff member came out of the back carrying a broom, a dustpan, and a small bucket. After cleaning up the mess, he took some rags from the bucket and wiped up the coffee and creamer. When he was finished, the floor was spotless and there was no sign of the accident—except for Hilda's red face.

"Hilda, go back and get their drinks again," Tilly said with a smile. "But this time let's put them on the table."

Several diners sitting nearby laughed and went back to their meals. Tilly had successfully dealt with the awkward situation.

Hilda scurried off, and Tilly leaned over the table. "Your meals are on me tonight."

"That's not necessary, Tilly," Joan said. "We weren't hurt in any way. An accident is an accident."

Tilly waved one of her manicured hands at the women. "You're good customers. I've been wanting to treat you for a while. Please allow me to do this. And don't order something cheap to save me money. I know what dishes you like, and I'll know what you're up to."

"That's very kind," Priscilla said with a smile. "Thank you."

"You're welcome."

"Before you go," Priscilla said, "would you sit with us a minute? I...we'd like to ask you something."

Tilly frowned, but she nodded and sat down. "What can I do for you?"

Priscilla cleared her throat while she thought about how to frame her questions. She didn't want Tilly to think she suspected her of anything, but she also wanted her to be candid. Finally she said, "Have you heard about the painting found in my cottage?"

Immediately Tilly's expression became guarded. "It's the talk of the town. Of course I've heard about it."

"We're trying to find out who painted over it and gave the painting to our aunt. I'm certain she had no idea the Adair work was under it."

"I agree. Your aunt was a very honest woman."

"I was told you were part of an artists' group a long time ago. About the time the painting was stolen. It was called the Tisbury Collective."

Tilly's eyes narrowed, and her mouth became a thin line.

Not wanting to alienate her, Priscilla quickly said, "Please understand we don't suspect you of anything. That would never occur to us. All we want is to find out how Marjorie got the painting."

The tightness in Tilly's face softened a little. "I don't know," she said. "I can tell you that things got very uncomfortable around the same time the painting went missing from Plymouth, but it had nothing to do with the theft. Your mother and Marjorie started having problems. I think it had to do with Billy Manders. Marjorie cared deeply for him at one time, but she always believed that your mother undermined that relationship. There was a big argument that summer. Then on Thanksgiving they had the blowout that ended it all. You and your parents never returned to the island after that. Until you moved here."

"Did anyone in the group talk about *Seascape in Shadows?*" Gail asked.

Tilly snorted. "Of course we talked about it. The theft was a big deal. The story was on national news, and we fancied ourselves artists." She smiled and shook her head. "I don't know what I was thinking. After the collective disbanded I never picked up a paintbrush again. I wasn't good. I think I was excited about the *idea* of painting."

"Tilly, Hilda saw a picture of *Seascape in Shadows* on my phone," Trudy said. "We were talking about the theft. When she saw the photo, she looked shocked and dropped the tray. Why would she do that?"

At first Tilly looked surprised. Then she laughed. "Oh, poor Hilda. I have a print of *Seascape in Shadows* in my house. She's been there, and I'm sure she saw it. If you were talking about a stolen painting and she saw this picture..."

Trudy grinned. "She thought you might be hiding a missing masterpiece?"

"Yes." Tilly covered her mouth with her hand. "She must not know it's been found. I shouldn't laugh, but it is a little funny." She smiled at the women. "If you don't have any other questions, I think I need to assure her I'm not a master art thief."

"By all means," Priscilla said. "And thank you for talking to us. If you think of anything else... anything that might help... please let one of us know."

"I will." She stood, sighed, and looked off into the distance as if seeing something the rest of them couldn't. "That was a long, long time ago, and I haven't thought about the collective for many years.

It's possible I might remember something that you'd find interesting, but I'll have to spend some time trying to revisit those years."

"There is one other thing," Priscilla said, deciding to take a chance and hope Tilly wouldn't close up again. "I understand a couple of the members have moved away. I don't suppose you know where they are? I was given the name Raymond Hill, but I don't know who the other person was."

Tilly's forehead wrinkled in thought. "Yes, I believe a couple of people are no longer in Tisbury. That would be Raymond Hill and Dora Metcalf." She smiled sadly. "Raymond and I used to be friends, but I was closer to Dora. I have no idea where Raymond is, but if I remember right, Dora moved to Wyoming. She has a daughter in Vineyard Haven, but I can't remember her name right now." She shook her head. "Billy Manders moved away too. Went to Colorado, I believe. He passed away almost ten years ago." She smiled sadly. "He was a nice man. I really liked him."

"Billy's dead?" Joan said. "Really? This is the first I've heard of it."

Tilly nodded. "He was very ill. I found out from Alma. She kept in touch with him after he left."

Priscilla snuck a look at Joan. So Alma had been keeping tabs on Billy? Maybe Trudy was right, and Alma did know more than what she was saying. They would probably have to speak with her again, but Priscilla wasn't the one to do it. Alma wasn't a very pleasant person, and Priscilla's relationship with her had been rocky. Since Trudy had already talked to her, maybe she could push Alma a little further.

Priscilla thanked Tilly again, and Tilly dashed off to check on other customers.

"Here comes Hilda," Trudy said in hushed tones.

Sure enough, the harried waitress was coming their way with another tray. Priscilla said a silent prayer that things would go differently this time.

"For goodness' sake," Gail hissed. "Don't say anything to upset her. I'd actually like my coffee in a cup instead of on the floor."

Trudy wrinkled her nose. "Funny."

Priscilla smiled at Hilda as she approached, hoping it would encourage her. Hilda looked tense, but she smiled back. When she reached the table and successfully removed the drinks from her tray, Priscilla had to fight back a sigh of relief.

"Hilda," Trudy said suddenly. "I take it you didn't know that the stolen painting had been discovered in Priscilla's house?"

Hilda shook her head. "I overheard some customers talking about a missing painting, but I didn't understand that it had been found. When you showed the picture on your phone, I realized Tilly had one just like it hanging in her house. I guess it just startled me." She looked around the table. "I'm sorry for my reaction. It was silly." She bit her lip and stared down at the floor for a moment. "I'm not myself right now. My husband, Leon, lost his job about a month ago. We recently took in our two grandchildren because our daughter is in the army. She's overseas, and we're not sure how long she'll be gone. We just can't tell her. She would worry." Hilda's cheeks turned pink, and she took a step back. "I-I'm sorry. I don't know why I shared that. Please forgive me. It's certainly not your problem." Before anyone at the table could respond, Hilda turned and hurried away.

The women were silent for a moment. Finally, Trudy said, "Well, we have to do something about that." The other three women nodded in unison.

"Where did Leon work?" Priscilla asked.

"Some hardware store in Edgartown," Joan said. "Hilda mentioned it once. I don't remember the name of the store."

"I was at Carter's in Vineyard Haven the other day," Trudy said. "Joe Carter mentioned that he was looking for someone. His kids have gotten really busy in school and can't help out as much."

"Maybe you could give him a call?" Priscilla said.

Trudy smiled. "Maybe I could. First thing in the morning."

"Until then, I think Hilda and Joe could use some help," Joan said. "How 'bout we put something together and send it anonymously?"

"I'm going to share this with Pastor Billings," Trudy said. "We have a pretty nice fund set aside to assist people in need. I'll bet he'd like to help."

Priscilla smiled at her cousins. She'd grown to love them more than she ever thought she could. She felt blessed to be related to them. She was also relieved to know she wouldn't be alone in trying to clear Marjorie's name. It might just take all of them to figure out what had happened. Could they really solve a mystery that began fifty years ago?

CHAPTER EIGHT

After dinner, Priscilla and her cousins talked a little more about the Adair painting and tried to figure out how to gather information that could lead them to the truth. Unfortunately, solving a fifty-year-old mystery wasn't going to be easy.

Priscilla was just getting ready to leave when her cell phone rang. When she pulled it out of her purse, she saw Gerald's name on her screen. She frowned at the phone for a moment and then declined the call.

"Anything wrong?" Joan asked.

Priscilla shook her head. "No. I can take care of it later."

Although Joan didn't say anything, Priscilla had a feeling she suspected who the call was from.

After thanking Tilly for their meal, the cousins walked out to the parking lot. Everyone said goodbye, and Gail and Trudy headed toward their cars. Only Joan stayed behind.

"Look, Priscilla," she said, her voice shaking a bit from the cold. "I don't want to get into your business, but I really think you need to tell Gerald how you feel about him. It might stop him from leaving town."

Priscilla shook her head. "I do have feelings for him, Joan, but they're not strong enough for that. I'm still mourning Gary. I'm not sure I'm ready to fall in love again."

Joan hooked her arm through Priscilla's. "Look, I'm not an expert on love, but I can tell you one thing. Love isn't always a choice. Sometimes it just happens. And when it does, chances are good it's because God sent someone your way. You need to give this to Him and let Him work it out. What if Gerald wants to stay? What if he wants to be with you, but he needs to know you don't want him to go? Shouldn't you at least find out?"

Priscilla squeezed her cousin's arm. "And what if he doesn't? What if I embarrass myself and him? I can't do it. Besides, I don't want to come between him and his daughter. Especially since we have no idea if a relationship between us would work. It would be selfish."

Joan sought Priscilla's eyes. "It's your decision, but I hope you're not making a mistake you'll be sorry for. Sometimes we have to take a chance, Priscilla. It's what life is all about. If we're not willing to be wrong, we may never know if we're right."

Priscilla laughed lightly. "I'm not sure that makes sense."

"You know exactly what I mean." Joan let go of Priscilla's arm and gave her a hug. "Call me if you need to talk. I'm here for you anytime."

"I know you are, and I appreciate it." Priscilla watched as Joan got into her car and drove out of the parking lot. Was Joan right? Should she tell Gerald how she felt? As soon as she asked herself the question, she dismissed it. She'd meant what she told Joan. She wasn't sure enough about her feelings to ask Gerald to give up living near his daughter. It would be incredibly selfish.

Priscilla climbed into her SUV and started the engine, waiting for it to warm up. Her phone rang again and once more she took it out of her purse. Gerald. She couldn't keep ignoring his calls. She started to answer, but at the last second, her finger hit the *Decline* button. She stared at her silent phone. Why had she done that? Ignoring him wasn't going to change anything. She put her phone back in her purse, deciding the next time he called, she'd answer. If she didn't, he might figure out she was purposely avoiding him.

Priscilla pulled out onto the road. She tried to think about something else, but thoughts of Gerald kept creeping into her mind.

She'd just left the lights of Tisbury behind and had turned onto the road that led to the cottage when another car came up behind her and began to follow closely. Priscilla slowed down and moved over a bit to give the driver room to go around her, but the car stayed where it was. Priscilla slowed down even more hoping the driver would get frustrated and pass her. But the car only seemed to draw closer.

"Would you back off?" she said out loud, her frustration growing. She put her hand up and waved toward the other driver, hoping he'd take the hint. He stayed where he was. Finally, Priscilla decided to pull off the road at a scenic spot near the cliffs a few yards ahead and let the fellow pass. But when she pulled into the space and put her car in park, the other driver followed her, right on her bumper. To her horror, she realized he wasn't stopping—he was trying to force her car toward the cliff. She'd put her car in park and now pushed as hard as she could on the brake, almost standing in a frantic attempt to stop her forward momentum. The driver of the vehicle—she could see it was a white van—flashed his lights to bright beam and laid on his horn as he revved his engine.

Tears were flowing down Priscilla's face when she heard the distant sound of a siren. She was shaking like a leaf, her heart racing. She looked in her rearview mirror and saw red and blue flashing lights. The driver of the van backed up, swung his vehicle onto the road, and took off. She thought quickly and put on her emergency blinkers. Somehow she had to stop the cruiser and get help before that crazy driver returned. Thankfully, the police car pulled up behind her and stopped. Priscilla started to get out of her car when she heard someone from the police cruiser say, "Stay in your car, and put your hands out the window where I can see them!"

CHAPTER NINE

Priscilla was so taken aback, she just sat there for a moment. The voice came again. "Put your hands out the window right now!" Not knowing what else to do, Priscilla rolled down her window, stuck her hands out, and waited. She watched the cruiser's door open and someone step out. What in the world was going on?

The officer approached slowly, and Priscilla could see that he had his hand on his holster. What was happening? As he approached, she sat still, not moving. She suddenly realized she was holding her breath. When he reached the window, she turned her face to look up at him. The expression on his face shook her to the core. Eyes hooded, mouth tight, the young policeman looked as if he'd just pulled over the most dangerous criminal in Massachusetts.

"I need you to get out of the car, Mrs. Grant," he said in a low voice. Something to her right caused her to jump. She swiveled her head to see another policeman peering into her car. She quickly turned back toward the first man. She recognized him as Officer Travis, a new addition to the island police force.

"Officer, what's going on? What are you doing?"

"Just get out of the car." He opened the door and took her arm, pulling her out and onto the road. Then he led her to the front of her car. "Will you just put both hands on the hood? And stay there. Don't move."

Priscilla's fear and frustration was turning to anger. She was being treated like a criminal—right after someone had frightened the wits out of her. Frankly, she'd had enough. She slowly put her hands down and turned to face the man. "Now listen here," she said, her voice shaking. "Someone just tried to push me off the cliff. Now you pull me over and act like I'm public enemy number one. This is ridiculous, and I'm not going to put up with it!"

Officer Travis took a step toward her as if he planned to force her to comply with his previous instructions. But at the last second he hesitated.

"Look, Mrs. Grant. I had to stop you. You don't have to put your hands on the hood of your car, but I do need you to step away from your vehicle. We need to search it."

"Search my car?" Priscilla stomped her foot out of annoyance. "You should be chasing after the person who just tried to kill me! I thought he just wanted to get around me, but when I pulled in here to let him pass, he followed me in and tried to push my car with his—does that interest you at all?"

Travis put his hands on his hips and scowled at her. "Actually, it does. But for now, I need you to sit in the back of my car while we search your SUV."

"Do you mind if I ask what you're looking for?"

Travis gestured to the second officer, who opened the passenger door of Priscilla's car. He leaned inside and began looking around.

"What do you think I have?"

"Someone broke into the police station and took your painting."

Priscilla couldn't believe her ears. It took her a few moments to digest this information. Finally, she said, "Let me get this straight. You let someone get away with a priceless painting? Why didn't you have it locked up? What kind of police station do you have?" Even though it was dark, Priscilla's headlights provided enough light for her to see the officer's complexion darken.

"A small station without enough people to patrol the streets and guard evidence, I guess," he said gruffly.

"And now you think I took the painting? I told you I had no idea the Adair was under my aunt's picture. I had no idea who Adair even was."

"You wouldn't have to. Once you knew its worth, you could have decided to get it back and sell it."

Priscilla put her hand on her hip. "Do I really look like an art thief? Seriously?"

"What you look like doesn't mean anything."

Priscilla sighed loudly. "Okay, okay. When was the painting taken?" She was trying hard to ignore the second officer's vigorous search through her car. She prayed he wouldn't damage her leather seats.

"About an hour and a half ago."

"Well, I was having dinner at the Inn with my cousins. We were there from seven until a little after nine. It would have been impossible for me to take it."

"The station isn't that far from the restaurant."

"But I never left my chair. You can ask my cousins, our waitress—and Tilly. She can confirm that I was there the entire time."

He frowned. "You can bet I'll check."

"Good," Priscilla said. "Then you can leave me alone and move on."

Travis fell silent as another squad car pulled up to the scene, lights flashing. Priscilla watched as Chief Westin stepped out and confronted the young officer. "Travis, what is going on here?"

The second officer slammed the door of the SUV and joined them. "She doesn't have it. There's nothing suspicious in her car."

"That's what I told you," said Priscilla, glaring at the man.

"Chief," Travis said. "We got an anonymous call to the station. Someone said Mrs. Grant had the painting. We were on our way to her house when we found her here, on the side of the road. I thought it best to search her car before she could get home and stash it somewhere."

The chief folded his arms across his chest. "Did it even occur to you that maybe the caller was trying to frame Mrs. Grant to get you off his tail and give him time to get away?"

"I didn't think of that," Travis mumbled. He walked over to Priscilla's SUV. He pulled a flashlight out of his belt and turned it on, examining her back bumper. "She says someone tried to push her off the cliff, Chief. I don't see any dents or scratches."

"He didn't ram me, he pushed me," Priscilla said. "It was a van, white, I think. I couldn't see the driver. All I could really see were its headlights in my rearview mirror—and a flash of the back of it as it drove away."

"Which way did it go?" Chief Westin asked.

Priscilla pointed at the road, away from town. "He just kept going. He's long gone by now, with all the time your officers wasted searching for something I told them I didn't have."

"Did you see a license plate? Even part of one?"

Priscilla searched her memory. Had she seen anything that might help? Something popped into her head. "There was something…some kind of decal in the back window, I think." She tried hard to bring up the image, but she couldn't. "I'm sorry, Chief. I just can't remember what was on the sticker. If I saw it again, I might recognize it."

"It would certainly help if you could do that. There are lots of white vans in town. Hard to narrow it down."

"I'll keep trying to recall it," Priscilla said, her teeth chattering. "Can I go now? I'm freezing."

He nodded. "If you suspect anyone of this theft, I need to know, Mrs. Grant. Don't keep important information to yourself. This person has tried to hurt you once, and if he thinks you know something that could implicate him…"

Priscilla couldn't take much more. "Chief, I just want to go home and get warm. I don't have any more idea of who to suspect than you do. Let's just remember I'm not the one who left it unguarded in the police station."

He exhaled sharply, his breath looking like smoke in the icy air. "First of all, I'm not happy about a famous painting being found in my town. And secondly, allowing it to be stolen isn't the crowning moment in my career. But mark my words. I will discover the truth."

"I'll be looking for that same truth," Priscilla said firmly. "I won't allow my aunt's name and reputation to be besmirched."

The chief took a step closer to her. "Just don't get in the way, Mrs. Grant. I mean it. I know you like to stick your nose into things. But this time you might be biting off more than you can chew."

If Priscilla wasn't certain Chief Westin was a good man, she would have felt a little intimidated. However, she recognized that this theft was personal to him, and he took it very seriously.

"Thank you, Chief. I'll remember that."

Priscilla turned away and got into her car. As she drove away, she was shaking, and it wasn't from the cold.

CHAPTER TEN

When Priscilla got home, she called Joan and told her about the white van and her encounter with Chief Westin. When she finished describing her experience, Joan was silent for a moment. Priscilla started to wonder if they'd been disconnected when finally, Joan said, "Why would anyone try to force you off a cliff, Priscilla? That's serious. You could have been badly injured. Even killed."

"I know that. Someone called the police station and told them I had the painting, Joan. I think they wanted the police to concentrate on me so they could get the painting out of town."

"Maybe..." Joan said slowly.

"It's the only thing that makes sense. I don't know anything, and I don't have the Adair. I'm hardly a threat to anyone."

"Unless someone thinks you are."

"But why?"

"I don't know, but we need to figure it out," Joan said. "I'm worried about you, Priscilla."

She wanted to dismiss Joan's concerns, but her experience on the road had shaken her. "Let's forget about the van for now," she said. "Who do you think took the painting?"

"Frankly, it could be anyone," Joan said. "The whole town knows how valuable it is. I think we need to follow up on the collective, but it might not be any of the past members. Anyone who knew the Adair was at the station could have broken in and taken it."

"But it would have to be someone who knows how to get rid of a priceless stolen painting."

There was another long silence. "You know," Joan said, "maybe it's the same person who took the painting in the first place. I mean, if they were acquainted with the black market when the painting was originally stolen, they probably still know how to get rid of it for a profit."

"But that was over fifty years ago, Joan."

"Most of the people in the collective are still around."

"I guess you're right." Priscilla sighed. "So, the person who took the painting fifty years ago might be the same one who took it today? Wow. That would be something, wouldn't it?"

"Could the person who tried to push you off the cliff be the thief?"

"I guess so, but I still have no idea why he'd do that."

"You're getting a reputation for solving mysteries, Priscilla. Maybe someone doesn't want you looking too closely at this. They're afraid you'll uncover the truth."

Priscilla was a lot more comfortable with the thought that the attack on her was carried out to misdirect the police. But what if Joan was right? The thought made her feel queasy. "Then they have a lot more confidence in me than I do. Besides, I don't do anything without all of you." Something occurred to Priscilla that made her gulp. "Maybe you, Trudy, and Gail should be careful. What if this nut decides to come after you?"

"My guess is that he won't try again. Especially since the police showed up. I bet he'll lay low. At least for now."

"That makes sense," Priscilla said. "I certainly hope you're right."

"The chief is probably checking out all the white vans in Tisbury and the surrounding area."

"I'm sure he is," Priscilla agreed. "I suspect that will be a long list." She heard a whine and looked down to see Jake sitting at her feet, obviously wanting to go out. "I need to go," she said to Joan. "Jake has to go outside, and I'm beat."

"You're going outside alone?" Joan asked, a trace of apprehension in her voice.

"No, I'm going outside with Jake," Priscilla said. "Trust me, he's a good watchdog. Besides, I thought you just told me that the driver of the van wouldn't risk coming after me again."

"No fair throwing my own words back in my face," Joan said. "Call me when you get back, okay? A little extra caution won't hurt."

"Okay. I'm going to hang up and take him out. I'll call you when we're back inside. Should be about fifteen minutes."

"Take your cell phone," Joan said. "That way if it's any longer I can call and check on you."

"Why don't I just call you on my cell and keep you on the line the entire time so you can hear me walking?"

"Maybe it would be best..."

"Oh, Joan, I'm kidding!"

"Very funny. Just call me when you're back inside and the doors are locked."

Joan disconnected, and Priscilla sighed as she hung up. First Joan said there was nothing to worry about, and then she seemed concerned about Priscilla being outside and unaccompanied. Was she safe or not? The whole thing seemed so silly. Priscilla wasn't a threat to anyone. Jake whined again, and she smiled at him. "Okay, let's go. I guess you're my protector now."

Jake barked like he understood her, causing Priscilla to chuckle. She got his leash and put it on him. Then she put on her coat, grabbed her cell phone, and opened the front door. Of course, no one was around, and she chided herself for being frightened. She and Jake stepped out into a cloudless night. The moon was bright, providing light for their walk. Although she glanced around more than once, everything was quiet.

Jake tugged at the leash, wanting to venture near the edge of the cliff. As they walked, Priscilla turned the evening's events over in her head. Who was in the white van, and what did they want? Joan's theory made some sense, but who would try to kill someone because they *might* figure out who you are and what you did? It seemed to Priscilla that no one would take such extreme steps unless there was some kind of real and dangerous threat. And there wasn't. She began to wonder if the person in the white van mistook her for someone else. Maybe it was a mistake. Was that possible?

"Jake, settle down." Jake's continued tugging at his leash was making her arm tired. "Let's go home." He'd already done his business, and she was exhausted. Again, he jerked the leash, and she realized that he was sniffing the ground. He seemed to have picked up a scent. Someone walking along the cliff. When he turned toward the house, his nose still to the ground, Priscilla began to worry. She relaxed her hold on his leash. He kept sniffing and pulling her toward the cottage. As they neared home, she realized Jake was tracking something between the road and her house. She had no idea how fresh the scent was. Or what—or who—it belonged to. They were almost to the cottage when Priscilla saw a vehicle on the road, headed right for them. She pulled hard on Jake's leash, trying to get him to hurry to the cottage, but he was determined to keep following the scent. Priscilla started to panic and pulled harder, almost dragging Jake behind her.

As the driver turned the large vehicle toward them, the headlights shone brightly, making it hard for Priscilla to see. Her foot got caught in a hole and she stumbled. Although she tried her best to stay on her feet, she fell to the ground. Jake hurried over to her, pushing her with his head as if trying to see if she was all right. Priscilla pushed herself up, trying to get to her feet, but pain shot through her ankle and she cried out. She heard something behind her and turned around. The silhouette of a man stood in front of her, outlined in his headlights. She couldn't see his face. As he got closer to her, she did the only thing she could think of and began to scream as loudly as she could.

CHAPTER ELEVEN

Priscilla! Priscilla, it's me! It's Gerald."

Priscilla stopped in mid-scream as Gerald knelt down and grabbed her by the shoulders. She was so relieved to see him, she started to cry. He lifted her up and wrapped his arms around her. She put her head on his shoulder while Jake barked at both of them.

When she pulled back, she said, "I'm sorry. I couldn't see your face. All I could see was some man coming at me."

"You thought someone was after you? But why? Is something wrong?"

The concern on his face almost made her start crying again. She leaned over and rubbed Jake's head to calm him, her fingers trembling. Jake finally stopped barking and licked her hand.

"Let's go inside," Priscilla choked out, "and I'll explain."

"Let me turn off the car," Gerald said. "I'll be right behind you."

Priscilla opened the front door and took Jake inside. She always left the front door unlocked when she walked Jake. She could see the cottage and felt safe leaving the door open. Until today, that is. Next time, she'd lock the door behind her and take her keys. She unhooked Jake's leash, but instead of running over and lying down in front of the fire, he continued sniffing the floor. He ran toward the kitchen and began to bark.

Just then the front door opened and Gerald came in.

"You want to tell me why you were afraid I was someone else?" he said.

"Yes, but could you do me a favor? Could you check the house? Make sure no one is here?"

Gerald frowned at her, but he nodded. "Of course, if you want me to."

She told Jake to be quiet, and he turned around and trotted over to where she stood. He sat down next to her, leaning against her leg. His devotion brought tears to her eyes. It was obvious he was worried about her. He wouldn't take his eyes off her face.

"I'm okay, Jake. Really." She ran her hands over his soft, furry head and smiled, hoping he would relax. It took a minute or two, but finally he trotted over to the rug in front of the fireplace and lay down.

Priscilla began to wonder if she should go ahead and call the police. Had she put Gerald in danger?

"Could you check the kitchen?" she asked Gerald after he'd checked the bedrooms.

"Sure." He walked into the kitchen and looked around. Then he came back to where Priscilla and Jake waited. "No one's in there. I'm going to check the attic next."

Priscilla watched as he went up the stairs. A couple of minutes later, he came down. "No one up there," he said. "I'll check the cellar and then come back here."

After a few minutes Gerald came back into the living room. "No one's here who shouldn't be, Priscilla. What's going on?"

She breathed deeply, trying to calm her shattered nerves. "I'll be happy to tell you. How about a nice cup of hot chocolate while I explain?"

"I guess so," he said hesitantly.

"Why did you come out here so late?" Priscilla asked.

"I've been worried about you," Gerald said, sitting down on the couch. "I heard about the painting. Everyone has, I guess. I was out this way and decided to see if you were up and felt like talking. I certainly didn't expect the reception I got."

Priscilla felt her cheeks warm. She couldn't imagine what he thought of her, screaming her head off like that. "I'm sorry," she said. "After I explain, maybe you'll understand."

"The explanation must be a doozy." He frowned. "I never saw you as a screamer, but you can out-squeal those actors and actresses in horror movies."

Although his words embarrassed her more than she already was, Priscilla couldn't help but laugh. "To be honest, I didn't know I could holler like that either." She shook her head. "I'm not usually a screamer, but with all the things going on lately...I guess I just reacted before I thought." She smiled at him. "I'll get our cocoa, and then I'll tell you the whole story."

She started to walk toward the kitchen when Gerald stopped her. "You're limping. Are you hurt?"

"No, I don't think so. I caught my foot in a hole. It's sore, but it's already feeling better. I'll be fine."

"Are you sure?"

She smiled and nodded. "I am. Just a temporary strain."

While he waited, she went into the kitchen and quickly fixed two cups of cocoa. Once they were ready, she took a can of whipped cream out of the refrigerator and topped off the drinks. Then she sprinkled a little cinnamon on top. Before taking the cups into the living room, she checked her ankle. The pain was almost gone, and there was no swelling. She was thankful it wasn't worse. Dealing with a broken ankle right now was something she didn't need. As she headed back into the living room, she tried to decide what to tell Gerald—and what to keep to herself. In the end, she decided to tell him everything. She really did trust him. No matter what, the last thing she wanted was to lose his friendship. She truly had come to depend on him.

"Here we go," Priscilla said, handing Gerald his cup.

"Thank you. I love hot chocolate," he said as he took it with a smile. "And you put cinnamon on it? Wonderful. Perfect."

Priscilla sat down in a chair next to the couch. After sipping her cocoa and trying to calm her nerves, she put her cup down on the coffee table. "So you heard about the painting?"

Gerald glanced up at the empty spot over the fireplace mantle. "I liked that painting. I'm going to miss it."

Priscilla sighed. "Me too. I only wanted it cleaned. Now all this is happening."

"All what is happening?"

Priscilla recounted her trip to the Art Attack and the visit from the chief earlier that day.

"Hank actually believes your aunt had something to do with the original theft? The one that happened fifty years ago? That's nonsense. Marjorie Latham wasn't a thief. One of the most honest, upstanding women I've ever met."

"I know that," Priscilla replied, "and so do the people who knew her. But I'm not sure the chief is convinced." Priscilla put her cup on the coffee table and crossed her arms over her chest. "I can't let people think something like that about her. I've got to find out what really happened. Who took that painting, and why it was in this house."

Gerald frowned. "I'm afraid that doesn't explain your reaction when I drove up. What happened to frighten you?"

Priscilla took a deep breath and blew it out quickly. "Coming home tonight someone in a van tried to push my car off the cliff. When I got home, I took Jake out. He seemed to be tracking something from the road to the house. With what happened tonight… Well, I was just reacting to that. Jake could have been sniffing anything. An animal, probably. My emotions were running high, and I was afraid whoever was in that van followed me to the house."

Gerald's eyes widened, and he put his cup down. "Someone tried to push you off a cliff? Are you serious? Why? I mean, you had nothing to do with the painting. You would have been very young when it was stolen. And you didn't even live here."

"I know that. Joan thinks he did it because he's the thief, and he's afraid of me for some reason. Maybe he thinks I know something that might compromise him. But of course, I don't."

"Maybe you do, but you don't realize it."

Priscilla shrugged. "I suppose that's a possibility."

"The chief needs to order some protection for you."

"I'm not sure I need to worry. I saw his van, and the police are searching for him. Approaching me again would be pretty stupid."

Gerald snorted. "You can't count on that, Priscilla. You're out here all alone. If you get into trouble, you might not be able to get help fast enough. What if that *wasn't* an animal outside?"

"I'm convinced it was, Gerald. This has happened before. I overreacted, I'm sure. I promise I'll be careful. If I feel at risk in any way, I'll call the police station immediately."

"And me, okay?"

Priscilla straightened up in her chair and picked up her cup. "That won't help me much when you're gone, will it?" She stared down at her cocoa, afraid to look at Gerald.

"Would it bother you if I moved away?" he asked softly.

"Of course it would. You're one of my closest friends. I don't know what I'll do without you." She finally dredged up the courage to meet his gaze. "Of course, your relationship with your family is more important. I don't fault you at all for leaving."

"Thank you. It's a hard decision, but I really want to be involved in my grandchildren's lives." He shrugged. "Again, it's only a possibility. There are other people up for the spot as well." He cleared his throat. "Let's get back to your situation. Do you have any idea who took the painting?"

Priscilla shook her head. "Not either time. Around the time it was stolen from the traveling exhibit, there was a group of local artists who met frequently in Tisbury. Called themselves the Tisbury Collective. Aunt Marjorie was part of that group. They broke up not long after the painting went missing. The only reason I'm looking more closely at them is because the painting ended up here."

"Who was in this group?" Gerald asked.

Priscilla named the members one by one. "There are two people who moved, and we found out that Billy Manders passed away. We know where most of the others are . . . except for their teacher, Adrian Deering."

"I can tell you where he is."

She looked at him in surprise. "Really? Do you know him?"

"Not really, but I've seen him. He lives at Harbor's Rest Nursing Home. Moved there a few months ago. Not long after his wife died."

Priscilla tried to digest this information. "But that's where Mildred's mother lives. She didn't tell me he was there."

"Are you sure she knows?"

"No. Even if she did, I didn't ask if she knew where Adrian was."

"Your mother and Marjorie fought over a guy named Billy, right? Could their tiff have anything to do with the painting?"

"My understanding is that their argument was over my aunt's attachment to Billy. She felt Mom came between them somehow." Priscilla rubbed her temples, trying to get rid of a headache that had crept up since the incident on the road. "I don't see how either one of them could have been involved with the painting," she said slowly. "I mean, my mother and Marjorie weren't the kind of people who would be involved in the theft of a valuable piece of art."

"Love can make people do things they wouldn't normally do."

Priscilla shrugged. "According to what my mother said, there wasn't anything between her and Billy except friendship. She tried to convince my aunt she was never interested in Billy romantically, but Marjorie didn't believe her. So why did they fight over him that summer? After Mom and Dad had been married for so long? Mom adored my father. The fight between Mom and Aunt Marjorie never made sense to me. I always felt there was something more to it."

"Why didn't Billy and Marjorie end up together?"

"I have no idea, but I can't imagine it had anything to do with what's happening now." Even as she said the words, Priscilla wondered if they were true. Maybe she should try to find out more about Billy Manders. Surely someone in the original group knew something about him. Gerald finished his cocoa and set his cup down on the table. "It's late, and I assume you're tired. Is there anything I can do to help you?" He patted the couch. "I can sleep here tonight if you want me to."

Priscilla smiled. This wasn't the first time he'd offered to sleep on her couch because he felt she needed protection. "No thanks, but I appreciate it. As I said, I doubt seriously whoever confronted me on the road will try again. Besides, I've got Jake here. He'll take good care of me. He always does."

Gerald stood, but his expression held doubt. "Just keep your phone charged and near your bed, okay? And call me if you suspect someone is outside."

Priscilla stood up as well. "Thanks, Gerald, I will. You have my word."

She walked him to the door and waved as he drove away. Before going back inside, she scanned the area once again, making certain no one was out there. She didn't see anyone, but she couldn't help wondering if her bravado in front of Gerald was more of an act than reality.

CHAPTER TWELVE

Wednesday morning dawned a little warmer than the day before. Priscilla checked the weather on her cell phone. Sure enough, the predictions said Massachusetts would move out of its cold snap, but they would have several days of rain, starting early today. Priscilla sighed. Cold to rain. The weather in Massachusetts was nothing if not unpredictable.

A quick check outside assured her that the rain hadn't yet begun. She called for Jake who was just finishing his breakfast. "We need to get outside now," Priscilla told him, "before the rain starts."

All Jake had to hear was the word *outside,* and he was ready to go. He ran over to the door. Priscilla got his leash, hooked him up, and they ventured outside. Thankfully, the warmer air was already here. Priscilla walked him, encouraging him to hurry. She didn't want to get caught in the rain. Jake didn't pick up any unusual smells, which made Priscilla feel better. When they made their way back to her front porch, she got him inside and unhooked his leash. "I know our walk seemed too fast," she told him, "but when it starts raining, you'll thank me."

Jake didn't respond, still looking a little perturbed that his time outside had been cut short. Priscilla was on her way to the kitchen when someone knocked on her door. A quick look at the clock showed it was barely eight in the morning. Who would stop by so early? Was Gerald so worried about her that he'd come back?

She opened the door and found two men she didn't know standing there. They both wore black suits.

"May I help you?" she said.

"Priscilla Grant?" one of the men said.

Priscilla nodded.

"I'm Special Agent Lonny Baxter from the FBI, and this is Special Agent Micah Peel. We're here about the painting you found. We have some questions. Could we speak to you for a few minutes?"

The first thing that popped into Priscilla's mind was *Mutt and Jeff*. Agent Baxter was tall and thin. Brown hair, brown eyes. Rather nondescript. Agent Peel was short with red hair, freckles, and bright green eyes. The two men couldn't be more different. Priscilla swung the door open. "Of course. Come in."

Although she was a little nervous about talking to the FBI, Priscilla had nothing to hide, so she tried to be as friendly as she could under the circumstances. She directed the men into her living room and offered them coffee, which they both accepted. They sat down on the couch. So far so good. They seemed relaxed. She went into the kitchen and made their coffee, then took it back into the living room.

"Cream or sugar?" she asked.

Both men shook their heads. "Black is fine," Agent Baxter said.

Priscilla sat down in a chair next to the couch. "You said you had questions. What can I do to help you?"

Agent Baxter sipped his coffee, then put the cup down on the coffee table while Agent Peel took a notebook and a pen out of his pocket. "We need to know how a painting by Arthur Melton Adair found its way into your home," Agent Baxter said. "Do you have any idea how that happened?"

"No," Priscilla said. "I had no clue there was another painting underneath mine. I took it in to be cleaned. It had gotten rather dingy. The shop contacted me and told me about the painting underneath it. I was really shocked."

"The picture belonged to your aunt? When did she acquire it?" Agent Peel asked.

"About fifty years ago. Someone gave it to her. Anonymously. Supposedly it was from a secret admirer. I just recently learned this. I'd always assumed she'd painted it. She was a talented artist."

"And that's all you know about it?" Agent Baxter asked as if she might be holding back information.

"Yes, I'm sorry. The painting was here when I inherited my aunt's property. I didn't know anything about its background."

"Who told you it was given to your aunt by this...secret admirer?" Agent Peel asked.

Priscilla didn't care for the way he'd framed his question. He emphasized the words *secret admirer* as if he didn't believe her.

"My cousin Joan. Aunt Marjorie told her about it."

Agent Baxter nodded. "Is there anything else you can tell us that might relate to the painting?"

Priscilla hesitated. Should she tell them about the collective? She really had no idea if they were involved, although it seemed odd that the painting would turn up in Tisbury and that the group would break up not long after that. But what if the agents contacted people who used to be in the group? Would they be angry with her?

"If you know something, Mrs. Grant, you need to tell us," Agent Baxter said.

"I'm not sure it's relevant," Priscilla said. "But around the time the painting was stolen, there was a group of artists that met in Tisbury during the summers. They called themselves the Tisbury Collective. My aunt was part of that group. I was told that not long after the painting went missing from Plymouth, something happened that caused a rift in the collective. Some people even left town." She shook her head. "It might mean nothing, but it makes me wonder if there could be a connection. I have to wonder if the person who gave her the painting was in the group."

"Do any of the members still live around here?" Agent Peel asked.

"Some of them are still in town. There are a few members who are no longer living or have moved away. I have to say that none of them appear to be the kind of people who would steal valuable art. Besides, who hides a painting worth as much as *Seascapes in Shadows* for fifty years? I mean, if they wanted to sell it on the black market, wouldn't they have done it long ago? The whole situation seems strange."

Agent Peel's eyebrow arched. "What do you know about the black market, Mrs. Grant?"

Priscilla laughed. "Nothing. Sorry. Something one of my cousins said. She says there are people who buy stolen art and keep it for themselves." She noticed the way the agents were staring at her, and she gulped nervously. "Not that I know anyone like that. I—I mean, I don't. It's just what she said..." Priscilla took a deep breath and tried to control her breathing. "Look," she said, struggling to keep her voice level. "I'm not a thief and neither was my aunt. I have no idea where that painting came from or who painted over it. I wish I could give you more information, but at this point, I've told you everything I know. If I find out anything else..."

"Mrs. Grant," Agent Baxter said firmly, "we need you to mind your own business. I don't mean to be rude, but interfering in our investigation won't be appreciated."

Priscilla had to bite her lip to keep back the retort on the tip of her tongue. She had no intention of *minding her own business.* Suspicion cast on herself, her aunt, or anyone in her family made it her business. She intended to keep digging for the truth, but instead of saying anything, she forced herself to nod and smile.

"We could use your help," Agent Peel said. "Could you please write down the names of anyone involved in this group who still lives in the area? And we'd like to talk to your cousins too. Can you also give us their names and addresses please?"

Priscilla didn't respond immediately. The last thing she wanted to do was to send the agents to harass her cousins or friends in town, but she realized their request was reasonable. Of course they'd have to talk to anyone related to Aunt Marjorie—who might know something about the painting. She wrote down the information the agents requested and handed it to Agent Peel. He glanced at it, then folded the sheet of paper and put it inside his notebook. As soon as the agents left, Priscilla planned to call her cousins and warn them. She wasn't sure what to do about the members of the collective. She didn't want them to blame her if the FBI showed up on their doorsteps.

Agent Baxter finished his coffee and stood up. Agent Peel put his notebook and pen back in his pocket and got to his feet.

"Thank you for your time," Agent Baxter said. "We need to ask you to stay in town. We might need to speak to you again."

"I don't plan to go anywhere," Priscilla said. "I'll be available whenever you need me."

After the agents left, Priscilla locked the door and leaned against it. Her heart thudded in her chest. She had great respect for the FBI. For all law enforcement. But she had to admit that being questioned by federal agents was a little unnerving.

She hurried over to the phone and quickly called Joan, telling her about the FBI's visit. Joan offered to call Gail while Priscilla phoned Trudy. Joan cautioned Priscilla against notifying any of the people from the collective about the FBI's visit. "You need to leave that alone, Priscilla. I know you feel guilty for mentioning them to those agents, but what if one of them *is* involved? You need to let the FBI deal with them."

Although Priscilla still felt bad, she realized Joan was right. "Okay," she said. "I'm going to call Trudy. You call Gail. I'll talk to you soon."

Joan said goodbye and hung up. Priscilla immediately called Trudy. When she finished telling her what had happened, Trudy made it clear she was upset.

"This is ridiculous," she spat out. "What is wrong with these people? How could we know anything about a theft that happened so many years ago?"

"Obviously, they don't suspect us of stealing the painting fifty years ago, but they think we might know who did. Or that we were aware of the real value of Aunt Marjorie's painting."

"But if you knew, why would you take it to be cleaned?" Trudy asked. "You'd have to be pretty dumb to take it to an art dealer when the truth could be uncovered."

Priscilla sighed deeply. "I know. Frankly, right now, I think they suspect everyone."

"So what's our next move?"

"I'm not sure, but I think I'm going to visit Adrian Deering. I want to find out what he knows."

"You know where he is?"

"Yes. Gerald told me he lives at Harbor's Rest Nursing Home," Priscilla said.

"That's where Mildred's mother lives," Trudy said.

"Yeah, but she certainly didn't tell me that. I find that a little odd, don't you?"

"I certainly do." Trudy paused. "Maybe we need to look a little closer at Mildred."

CHAPTER THIRTEEN

When she ended her call with Trudy, Priscilla called Joan back to see if she wanted to go with her to the nursing home. When Joan agreed, Priscilla made arrangements to pick her up around ten.

Priscilla hung up the phone and sat and drank her coffee while she thought about Mildred. Surely she knew Adrian was in Harbor Rest Nursing Home. Why hadn't she said something? Did Mildred know more than she was letting on?

Priscilla had just finished her coffee when a rumble of thunder shook the cottage. Jake looked up from his nap and stared at Priscilla.

"It's okay," she said soothingly. Jake didn't like thunder, and leaving him alone during a thunderstorm was something she didn't want to do. "If it keeps up, you can come with me. I know Joan would love to see you."

Even though she was sure Jake couldn't actually understand her, he seemed to accept her reassurance and put his head down. Of course, he'd have to wait in the car while she was inside the nursing home. If worse came to worst, Joan could wait in the car with him. She grabbed her phone and quickly brought up the weather report again. Thankfully, it looked like the thunder wouldn't last long. If it was gone by the time she got ready to leave, she'd let Jake finish his nap.

Priscilla got up and walked to the bedroom. Another clap of thunder made her jump. It promised to be a wet, chilly day so she picked out a pair of black corduroy slacks and a dark green sweater. When she pulled the sweater out of the closest she remembered the last time she'd worn it. Gerald had complimented her. "That sweater brings out the green in your eyes," he'd said with a smile. "You have lovely eyes." Priscilla's eyes were blue-green, like her mother's. She'd never thought of them as *lovely*, but ever since Gerald's comment, she'd begun to pay more attention to them. A little mascara and a dusting of eye shadow seemed to help highlight them.

"Priscilla Latham Grant," she said to her reflection in the mirror. "What are you doing? Stop it." She started to put the sweater back but then pulled it out again. She wasn't likely to see Gerald today. Besides, what if she did? It wouldn't do any good to worry about what *might* happen.

She sighed as she pulled the sweater over her head. Maybe she was wrong. Was she being selfish? She'd left her home for a new life. Maybe it was time to cut Gerald some slack. It was possible he simply wanted to watch his grandkids grow up as he said. Nothing wrong with that. She had to quit thinking about him. She had other things on her mind, and she needed to concentrate on them. Of course, the heart doesn't usually respond well to logic. It seems to have a mind of its own. All she could do was try to move on. That's what she'd been doing every day since Gary died.

When she was through dressing, Priscilla went out into the living room. She quickly checked the weather again. As predicted, the thunder seemed to have moved out, leaving behind a sky full of clouds and a slow, steady rain.

"So do you want to come with me?" she asked Jake.

He glanced toward the window where the rain dripped down the panes of glass, grunted, and put his head down.

"I take it that's a no?" Priscilla went to where Jake sat near the hearth and rubbed his ears. "I think the thunder is past, but if it comes back, stay calm. I'll be home soon."

Although he didn't acknowledge her comment, his tail thumped, letting her know he liked the attention.

Priscilla grabbed her raincoat and umbrella and ran out to the car. She pulled up in front of Joan's house precisely at ten. She tapped the horn, and the front door opened. Joan ran to the car and quickly slid inside, holding her umbrella out the door and shaking it until she felt it was dry enough to put inside the car.

"If it's not freezing, it's raining," she said by way of greeting.

"I know." Priscilla smiled at her. "Thanks for agreeing to come with me."

Joan grinned. "Wouldn't miss it. I want to find out what's going on as much as you do."

"Good. Then you can tell me what in the world I should say to Adrian Deering. How do we explain our visit? If he knows something about the painting, asking him directly would be a mistake. I've been running scenarios through my head on the way over here, but nothing sounds right."

Joan snorted and gazed at Priscilla with narrowed eyes. "Let me get this straight. We're on our way to talk to this guy and you still don't know what to say?" She shook her head. "Not like you. Right now, you're acting more like Trudy."

Although everyone loved Trudy, Joan's comment wasn't a compliment. Trudy was scatterbrained. And Joan was right. Usually, Priscilla would have figured out exactly how to approach Mr. Deering before she took off for the nursing home. Another sign that thinking about Gerald was making her nuts.

"Sorry," she said slowly. "I've had something else on my mind."

Joan reached over and put her hand on Priscilla's arm. "I know. Look, Priscilla. If you and Gerald are meant to be together, God will work it out. You don't need to worry about it. And if you're not…"

Joan didn't finish her thought, and she didn't need to. She was right. "I've got to release this to God," Priscilla said softly. She smiled at Joan and patted her hand. "Thanks for reminding me, Joan."

"You're welcome. I think you and Gerald are good for each other, but God can see things we can't. Gerald might not be the man He has for you."

"Maybe he doesn't have anyone for me. Maybe I'm supposed to stay single." She felt her eyes get moist. "I had a wonderful marriage. Perhaps we only get so much happiness in one lifetime."

Joan took her hand from Priscilla's arm. "You don't believe that. God loves you. He's your Father, and He wants you to be happy. Do you think He counts your blessings and crosses your

name off some kind of list when you've had all the joy you're enti-
tled to? Of course He doesn't. If what's best for you is to be with
Gerald, then it will happen. If not, either someone else will come
along, or you'll find joy in being single."

Priscilla smiled. "Guess I'm feeling sorry for myself. Not a
place of strength."

"Just because I'm happy the way I am, don't think I've decided
to stay single forever. I keep that door open. You never know what
God has around the corner."

Priscilla nodded and started the car. "I can celebrate the life I
had—and still enjoy the life I have now. God will take care of the
future." She wiped away a tear that rolled down her cheek. "Now
let's get to the nursing home while Adrian Deering is still alive."

Joan laughed. "Good idea. After we come up with a good reason for our visit."

Priscilla shrugged. "How about the truth? We have questions
about a painting. We're wondering if Mr. Deering might know
anything about it."

Joan looked skeptical. "Everyone knows about the Adair painting. Won't that sound like we think he might be involved in the
theft?"

"I'm not convinced *everyone* knows about it. I mean, people in
a nursing home probably aren't up on the latest Tisbury gossip."

"Maybe..." Joan said. "How about this? Mr. Deering was
your mother's art teacher, and you wanted to meet him so you
could find out more about her." Joan peered closely at Priscilla.
"Did you know your mother was artistic?"

Priscilla shook her head. "No. Not at all. She always claimed she couldn't even draw stick figures. I have no idea why she'd be in an art class."

"That's strange, isn't it? I wonder why she never told you. And you never knew she was part of the collective?"

"No. Of course, I was a child. All I wanted to do was play with my cousins and enjoy the summer. I had no idea where my parents were when they weren't with me. Do you remember anything about it?"

"No. Same as you. I simply wasn't paying attention."

Priscilla sighed. "Why is it so disconcerting to find out things about your parents you never knew?"

Joan shrugged. "Because they're our parents. They're not supposed to have their own lives."

Priscilla snuck a quick look at her. "I think you're right. I imagine our kids feel the same way." The idea that her mother might have been involved in the theft of the Adair hadn't occurred to Priscilla until that moment. Her hands tightened on the steering wheel. When they began to cramp, she loosened her hold. Would investigating the theft of *Seascape in Shadows* uncover something Priscilla would regret finding out?

CHAPTER FOURTEEN

About twenty minutes later they pulled up in front of Harbor's Rest Nursing Home. It looked like most other nursing homes—one level, with apartments stretching out on both sides of the main entrance. But at Harbor's Rest, the grounds and the building were very well maintained. The attention to detail and the obvious care given to the facility was a tribute to the leadership and the staff. The home had a good reputation. Priscilla was certain Adrian received quality care here.

She and Joan got out of the car, opening their umbrellas to protect themselves from the steady rain that still fell. When they got to the main entrance, they opened the door and stepped into a small lobby. The woman at the desk asked them who they were there to see.

Priscilla wondered if she should have cleared her visit beforehand. The nursing home was probably careful about who they let in. "We're here to visit Adrian Deering."

The woman stared at Priscilla over the tops of the thick black glasses that sat on the edge of her nose. "Did you say Adrian Deering?"

Priscilla nodded.

"He doesn't get a lot of visitors," the woman said. "Is he expecting you?"

"No," Priscilla said. "He doesn't know me. He taught art to my mother years ago. I just wanted to meet him."

The woman smiled. "I'm sure he would enjoy that." She pressed a button and the door behind them swung open. "Mr. Deering is in room 113," she said. "Take a left when you go through the door. You'll find it."

"Thank you." Priscilla headed for the door, and Joan followed her. Once they were both through it, Priscilla grabbed Joan's arm.

"I'm surprised she let us in," she said. "I mean, what if we were ax murderers or something?"

Joan giggled nervously. "We don't look like murderers, and we don't have axes. I don't think she considered that possibility."

"Well, regardless, I'm glad she let us through."

"Maybe some residents have an open-door policy," Joan said. "You know, anyone who shows up can be let in."

Priscilla considered Joan's comment. "Maybe. I got the feeling she was happy someone was here to see Mr. Deering, didn't you?"

"Yeah, I did. As if someone showing up to see him was unusual."

"That's what I thought." Priscilla checked a nearby sign on the wall, trying to find room 113. "Well, we're in the building. Let's see this through."

"Okay," Joan said. "But why do I feel like a mouse being lured into a trap?"

Priscilla lightly slapped Joan's arm. "Stop that. You're going to make me so nervous I might run back to my car, drive home, and leave you here!"

Joan grinned. "No you won't. I know you. You're as curious as I am."

"You're right," Priscilla said, smiling. "Besides, what's the worst that can happen? If he doesn't know anything about the missing painting, at least we'll make a new friend."

"Is your middle name Pollyanna?" Joan asked.

Priscilla rolled her eyes. "Sometimes."

They walked down the hallway, watching the room numbers. When Priscilla saw 113 she pointed it out to Joan. The rabid butterflies in her stomach calmed down, and she took a deep breath. "Here we go." She shot a look at Joan. "Back me up in there."

Joan's eyes widened. "Back you up? How? What does that mean? I'd sing 'la, la, la' in the background if it would help. Otherwise, I'll just smile and nod, if you don't mind."

Priscilla sighed. "Never mind. Just don't…"

"Suddenly yell out, 'We think you might know who stole a famous painting. Cough up the information?'"

"No, of course not," Priscilla said a little more crossly than she wanted to. She grabbed Joan's arm. "I'm sorry. The past couple of days have me on edge."

"I totally understand," Joan said. She held three fingers up in a gesture reminiscent of a Girl Scout salute. "I promise not to do anything to embarrass you or reveal our true mission." Then she saluted Priscilla. "I've got your six. We can do this."

"Now you're going to make me laugh. Stop it."

"I'm sorry."

"Okay." Before she could chicken out, Priscilla reached up and knocked on the door. A few seconds later a man swung it open. This couldn't be Adrian Deering. He was about six feet tall. Dark, straight hair, a round face...and looked to be about fifty years old.

"I-I'm sorry," Priscilla said, stumbling over her words. Was this the wrong apartment? "I'm looking for Adrian Deering."

The man smiled. It was then she realized he was wearing a shirt with the name of the nursing home on it. Must be an aide.

"He's here," the man said, pulling the door open. "Come in, ladies."

Priscilla stepped inside a tidy apartment. It was small, but it seemed to have everything someone might need. A small kitchen to the right as you came in. A short entry hall led to the living room. She noticed an open door also on the right, after the mini-kitchen. It was a bedroom with an attached bathroom. She swung her attention back to the man sitting in a recliner in the living room. He was tall and thin, with longish gray hair and a lined face framed by bushy gray eyebrows that needed to be trimmed. He wore dark slacks and a soft blue sweater with slippers on his large feet. He looked very comfortable.

Priscilla walked closer and held out her hand. "Mr. Deering? I'm glad to meet you. My name is Priscilla Grant. I believe you knew my mother? Charlotte Ingerson?"

The man took her hand and smiled, making Priscilla feel much more relaxed.

"Charlotte?" he said. "Where have you been? I thought you'd visit me before now. Why did you wait so long?"

Priscilla froze, her hand still in his. She had no idea what to say. As she slowly pulled her hand away, she felt someone touch her shoulder. She turned to see the man who'd let them in standing behind her.

"I need to talk to you just a minute," he said softly. "Will you step over here?"

She dumbly followed the man, trying to figure out what had just happened. When they were out of earshot, the man stepped up close to her. "I'm Preston Smith," he said in a low voice. "I work here, and I help Mr. Deering out as much as I can."

"Why does he think I'm my mother?" Priscilla asked. "She died some time ago."

Preston nodded. "Mr. Deering has lost the last forty-five years of his life."

"Does he have Alzheimer's? Or dementia?" Priscilla asked.

"Possibly. Or it might also have something to do with his inability to accept his wife's recent death. He doesn't remember her at all. Maybe it's his mind's way of protecting him against the pain of losing her. Unfortunately, he doesn't remember his children either. They tried to take care of him, but since he didn't know who they were, he was afraid of them. Kept telling them to get out of his house. For his own safety, they brought him here. He's happy and content now. I guess that's all we can hope for in the short term." He peered into Priscilla's eyes. "We pretend right along with him since we're not equipped to deal with his condition. He has a therapist who's trying to help him. We leave his treatment to her."

"So you're encouraging me to do the same? Pretend I'm my mother?"

He nodded. "If you could. I know it's awkward."

Priscilla glanced over at Joan who stood a few feet away. "We'll do whatever is best for Mr. Deering." She frowned at Preston. "He used to know my mother, and I wanted to ask him some questions. Now I'm not sure if I should."

He folded his arms across his chest. "I don't see why not. Just remember if it's something that happened during the last forty-five years or so, he won't be able to help you. And you'll have to interact with him as your mother."

Priscilla considered her options. If she didn't go along with this, she wouldn't learn anything from Adrian Deering. How badly did she want to solve this mystery? After thinking about her Aunt Marjorie, she squared her shoulders and straightened her back.

"All right, I'll try it," she told Preston. "As long as you don't think it will harm him in any way."

"It won't harm him. In fact, finally getting a visit from a friend might be just the thing he needs."

Priscilla bit her lip as she stared at her mother's former art teacher. *A visit from a friend? More like a visit from a ghost.*

CHAPTER FIFTEEN

After taking Joan aside and whispering in her ear, explaining what she was getting ready to do, Priscilla sat down on the couch next to Adrian's recliner.

"I'm sorry I didn't come to see you before now, Mr. . . . I mean, Adrian," she said softly.

He reached over and patted the hand she'd rested on the arm of the couch. "That's okay, Charlotte. I don't hold a grudge, you know. I'm just missing my friends. I'm so glad to see you."

"I'm glad to see you too."

"Skippy," Adrian said, looking over at Preston, "could you get us some tea? I'm parched, and I'm sure these lovely ladies would like some refreshment."

"Certainly, Adrian. I'd be glad to," Preston said. He looked at Priscilla. "Would you like a glass of tea?"

Priscilla nodded but Joan declined. She'd finally sat down in a small chair on the other side of the room. The dazed look on her face made Priscilla want to giggle, but Adrian Deering's condition certainly wasn't humorous. Running from the reality of loss was something she could relate to. Thank God she'd been able to find a new start. Not dealing honestly with pain was more tempting than most people realized.

"So, Charlotte," Adrian said, leaning toward her a bit, "what are you up to? Have you been sketching?"

Priscilla swallowed hard. Now what? She didn't want to lie, but neither did she want to cause Adrian confusion or distress. "Not too much," she said slowly. Since she actually did scribble little pictures in the margin of notebooks from time to time, she decided it could loosely be called *sketching*.

Adrian shook his finger at her. "You keep it up. You have real talent. You just need to develop it. And quit comparing yourself to your sister. Marjorie has a natural gift, but you're both good artists." He made a clucking sound with his tongue. "Siblings. Why can't they get along? My brother and I were just like you. But when he died, I realized we never argued about anything important. Just petty things. Things we should have let go. Of course, now it's too late." His voice broke on the last word.

"I'm sorry," Priscilla said gently. "I don't know why Marjorie and my m—I mean, why Marjorie and I fight so much. Why do you think that is?"

"Well, first of all, you were both too close to Billy Manders. Of course, you're married now, and he wasn't really interested in Marjorie even though I know she had a crush on him."

"Billy and I were just good friends," Priscilla said. Since she didn't know anything else about Billy, she hoped he wouldn't ask her a question she couldn't answer.

"He's very talented too," Adrian said. His forehead wrinkled, and he stared at her from hooded eyes. "Whatever happened to your sketches? You know, the ones you did before our little group disbanded. They were excellent."

"I'm not sure where they are right now, Adrian," Priscilla said.

He shook his head. "I hope you haven't lost them. They were very good. Maybe needed a little work on the perspective. You've got a good start though."

Where are the sketches now? Priscilla would go through her mother's trunks as soon as possible. She wanted to see the kind of art she used to create. She was discovering a whole new side of her mother. "Thanks," she said. Priscilla glanced over at Joan who finally seemed a little more relaxed. What should she ask next? Before she could make a decision, Joan broke in.

"Tell me about her sketches, Adrian," Joan said. "Which were your favorites?"

Adrian frowned at Joan. "Now, Alma, you know the ones I liked. We talked about it the last time we were all together, remember?"

Joan's mouth dropped open, and Priscilla almost lost it. Adrian thought Joan was Alma Whitaker? She was one of the most cantankerous people in Tisbury. And not attractive. She had a face like a hawk. Priscilla was certain Joan hadn't taken Adrian's confusion as a compliment.

"I don't remember," Joan said through gritted teeth. "Sorry."

Adrian smiled magnanimously. "Not a problem. Not everyone has the kind of memory I do."

Priscilla bit her lip again, not risking a look at Joan. "That's true," she said. "I have to admit that I'm not sure I remember either."

Adrian clicked his tongue several times. It sounded like *tsk, tsk, tsk.*

Before he had a chance to finish his thought or answer Priscilla's question, Preston brought a glass of iced tea into the living room and handed it to her.

She quietly thanked him as Adrian said, "Thank you, Skippy. I truly appreciate it." He nodded at Priscilla. "Skippy is such a blessing. I'm not sure how long I'll be here, but he comes by to help me whenever he can. That's a true friend. Not everyone deserted me."

Priscilla got the feeling the last comment was directed to her. She tried to look properly chastised.

Preston smiled at him and patted his shoulder. "Helping you is my pleasure."

Priscilla had a momentary desire to make a face at the helpful aide, but she realized how childish that was. She reminded herself that this wasn't a competition. She wasn't her mother and had nothing to feel guilty about.

Adrian scooted forward in his chair and winked at Priscilla. "I'm just here for a little rest, you know. Before long I'll go home. Right, Skippy?"

"Sure, Adrian," Preston said.

Priscilla glanced over at Preston, who shook his head so slightly Adrian didn't notice. It was obvious Adrian was here to stay. Priscilla wondered what the Skippy moniker was about. Must be his nickname. Not a great nickname for a manly man. Of course, Skippy seemed to be Adrian's golden child right now. She was clearly second choice.

"So tell me about the rest of our group," Adrian said. "How's Marjorie? And what's Billy doing? And what about Tilly?"

Priscilla just stared at him. Thankfully, Joan saved the day.

"Charlotte and Marjorie don't fight about Billy anymore," Joan said tactfully. "Billy left town, and Tilly is…working in a local restaurant. We see her when we can."

Priscilla smiled gratefully at Joan. This was getting ridiculous. She needed to find a way to ask the questions she'd come here to ask. Adrian's condition had thrown her for a loop. "Adrian," she said, "did you hear about the theft of *Seascape in Shadows* by Arthur Melton Adair?"

Adrian frowned at her for several seconds, as if trying to grasp a memory that was trying its best to fly away. Finally, he said, "Yes. Now that you mention it, weren't we talking about that the last week we met? It's hard to remember. Almost five years ago now, isn't it? If I recall correctly, it was shortly before you and Marjorie had that awful argument about Billy."

"I think you're right," Priscilla said. "It was a terrible loss. Beautiful painting."

Adrian nodded. "Adair was a master at catching the majesty of New England—especially our seacoast."

"Yes. Yes, he was," Priscilla said. "Did it seem to you that… Well, that some of the people in our group…knew something about that painting?"

For the first time since they'd arrived, Adrian's expression became guarded. "I don't think we need to talk about that. No one in our group would steal another artist's work. Not even…" He caught his breath and looked away.

Frustrated, Priscilla decided to push him. Just a bit. "Where was everyone when the painting was stolen?" she asked. "Was anyone in Plymouth when the Adair went missing?"

Adrian's look of disapproval deepened. "We need to change the subject," he said firmly. "I can't tell you anything about that. Let's talk about something else." He looked down at the floor for a moment. When he looked up again, his smile had returned. "I remember. We were talking about your sketches, Charlotte." He trained his watery blue eyes on her. "How are you coming along with the sketch of the Latham cottage and lighthouse?"

CHAPTER SIXTEEN

Priscilla was so dumbfounded by Adrian's question that she couldn't come up with a response. She flicked her gaze over to Joan, who looked like she'd been slapped in the face. It wasn't possible. Surely it was just a coincidence. Priscilla's mother would never be involved in the theft of a valuable painting. The idea was ludicrous.

"It's going okay, I guess," Priscilla said finally.

"I hope you finish it. I think it will make a lovely painting." He shook his finger at her. "Maybe you could give it to your sister. You know, extend it as a peace offering. I think it would mean a lot to her."

"I'll think about it." Not knowing what else to do, Priscilla stood up. "I'm sorry, Adrian, but we've got to be going. I hope it's okay if we come back to see you."

"Of course," he said, his eyes shiny with excitement. "I've missed you, Charlotte. And you too, Alma. Maybe you could bring some of the others with you. We could have a reunion."

Priscilla nodded quickly, feeling guilty. "Sure. I'll see what I can do."

He fixed his gaze on her. "You need to make up with Marjorie. Someday, she'll be gone, and it will be too late to make up."

"Thanks, Adrian," Priscilla said. "I'm sure you're right."

Adrian smiled at her and then turned his attention to Joan, who had also gotten to her feet. "You come back too, Alma, okay? You were always one of my favorite students. Always so sweet-natured. I can see you haven't changed."

Once again, Priscilla had to avoid looking at Joan. If Alma was ever sweet-natured, Priscilla and Joan hadn't seen it.

"Thank you, Adrian," Joan said. "I'm sure we'll see you again soon."

As the two women headed for the door, Preston, who had been cleaning up the dishes in Adrian's small kitchen, followed them. He pointed toward the door and put a finger up to his lips.

Priscilla and Joan stepped out into the hallway. Preston came out behind them and pulled the door shut.

"That was great," he said, smiling at them. "I know it's difficult to pretend, but if you try to correct someone suffering from this kind of dementia, it can confuse them. Frighten them."

"I imagine it would," Joan said. "If someone told me I'd lost over forty years of my life, it would distress me to no end."

"He hasn't had any visitors lately," Preston said. "He doesn't have much family left, and those he has he doesn't remember. It's very hard for them to carry on a conversation with a man who thinks they're strangers."

"That must be why the woman at the front desk looked surprised when we said we were here to visit him," Priscilla mused.

Preston nodded at Priscilla. "Exactly. I really hope you'll come back. He needs to be around people. Something someone says or does might trigger his memories."

"But then he'll remember that his wife is gone," Priscilla said. "I'm not sure he'll be any happier."

"That's true," Preston replied, "but not facing reality... Well, it's not healthy. He needs to confront his grief so he can truly heal. Right now, he's simply ignoring the pain."

"We're trying to get some information from him," Joan said. "About a missing painting. It's as if he remembers something that might be important but he doesn't want to say it."

Preston nodded. "That's how it works, unfortunately. I can't guarantee he'll ever tell you what you want to know. But you seem good for him. He hasn't engaged that much with anyone for a while."

"Because he thinks we're someone else," Priscilla said. "He certainly likes you. Are you assigned to him specifically?"

Preston shook his head. "No. I work all over the facility. I just like doing what I can for Adrian. He's a really nice guy."

"Why does he call you Skippy?" Joan asked. "Is that your nickname?"

Preston laughed. "No, it isn't, thank goodness. I have no idea why he calls me that. I have to admit I'm not fond of it, but if it makes him happy, I can endure it, I guess."

"Well, God bless you for keeping an eye on him and helping him so much," Priscilla said. "He's a fortunate man."

Preston actually blushed. "Thank you, but I try to treat everyone here with respect. Most of these people have lived long, productive lives. Unfortunately, when they come here, families tend to stop by infrequently. It's sad."

Priscilla smiled at him. "I guess we'd better get going."

"Did talking to him help you at all?" Preston asked.

Priscilla paused. She hadn't learned anything about the Adair painting, but that wasn't the reason she'd told Preston they were there. "Actually, it did. I never knew my mother sketched. I was surprised when I learned she was part of Adrian's art class. She never talked about any interest in art. I wanted to know more about that side of her."

"Well, I hope your trip was worth it then."

Joan slipped her arm through Priscilla's. "No matter what, I feel as if we made a friend."

Priscilla suppressed a giggle at Joan's attempt to throw her own words back in her face.

"You made his day. Thank you, ladies." Preston smiled and went back into the apartment.

Priscilla hurried down the hallway. Although Harbor's Rest Nursing Home was a nice, clean, and well-kept facility, she was starting to feel as if the walls were closing in on her. Joan scurried to keep up with her, but she didn't say anything until they got outside. Then she grabbed Priscilla's coat sleeve. They stood under the large metal canopy that shaded the front entrance and kept them dry from the steady rain that fell around them.

"Priscilla," Joan said, "just because your mother was drawing the cottage and lighthouse, it certainly doesn't mean she's the one who painted over the Adair."

"You have to admit it sounds suspicious."

Joan shook her head. "No, it doesn't. The Latham property is one of the most well-known places in the Vineyard. It's been sketched and painted many, many times. I'll bet Adrian asked everyone in the class to draw it."

Priscilla was stopped short by Joan's comment. "You—you might be right. I've had several groups stop by and ask if they could sketch my property. Even the local high school. I've got a guy now who's trying to capture it. Unfortunately, the weather hasn't been cooperating with him." She glanced back at the entrance door. "Maybe I should ask Adrian more about..."

"No, not now. We need to remember that he's a very confused man. Rushing back in there and questioning him about some assignment fifty years ago might unsettle him. We'll come back in a few days and ask him in a way that won't bewilder him even more."

Although Priscilla wanted to get the information from Adrian now, she realized that Joan was right. They really had no idea how emotionally fragile Adrian was. Pushing him too much might cause a problem they couldn't fix. That wouldn't do him—or them—any good.

"Okay. You're probably right about the assignment being for everyone, but when he said that about Mom drawing the cottage and the lighthouse, it shocked me. I think finding out about her interest in art has left me a little unsure. Why wouldn't she ever mention it? I thought I knew everything about her."

"My guess is, she wasn't very good and didn't feel confident showing you her work."

"If she was responsible for the painting that hung over my fireplace, she was pretty talented."

"But again, we don't know that she was responsible for it."

Priscilla sighed. "You're right, I guess."

"Good," Joan said. "Do you feel any better?"

"I guess so. I need to stop jumping to the worst-case scenario."

"I agree." Joan took her umbrella out of her bag and clicked it open. "Let's brave the rain and have lunch."

"Sounds good."

They were just preparing to run to Priscilla's SUV when her cell phone rang.

"Wait a minute," Priscilla said. She opened her purse and pulled out her phone. It was Trudy, and she sounded upset.

"Trudy, you've got to calm down," Priscilla said. "I can't understand you." The rain was coming down harder, making it difficult to hear.

"I said, the FBI just left here, Priscilla. They asked me all kinds of questions about Marjorie...and you. They seem to believe you have the Adair painting!"

CHAPTER SEVENTEEN

After trying to settle Trudy down some, Priscilla told her to call Gail. Gail worked as a dental hygienist, but could usually get away for lunch. Priscilla told Trudy to meet her and Joan at the cottage. When she hung up she told Joan, "I hope it's okay if we go to my place. Trudy is pretty upset. I'm not sure this conversation should take place in public."

"It's fine with me, but do we need to pick up something for lunch?"

Priscilla smiled. "I just made a big batch of chicken salad with red grapes and walnuts. You know me. I always make too much. If you're willing to eat chicken salad sandwiches and fruit, I've got it covered."

Joan smiled. "Your chicken salad? Sounds wonderful. It's one of my favorite foods."

"I even baked some brownies. I think we'll be fine."

The women raced to the car, got in, and headed to Priscilla's cottage. Although Joan was going over their visit with Adrian, Priscilla only half-listened. What did Trudy mean by saying the FBI thought she had the Adair painting? Was this just Trudy overreacting again? Or did they really suspect Priscilla of being involved in the theft? It was ludicrous. What kind of proof could they have?

This was getting crazy. Priscilla had a lot of respect for law enforcement and assumed the FBI wouldn't accuse her unless they had good reason. Although she tried not to worry, she couldn't help feeling concerned.

As if she were reading Priscilla's mind, Joan said, "Don't take what Trudy said too seriously. You know how she exaggerates things when she gets upset. I'm sure the FBI doesn't think you're hiding that painting."

Priscilla snorted. "You know me too well. I certainly hope you're right. I mean, I did know the painting was valuable before it went missing. Maybe they think I came back to get it after learning the truth."

"If that's the case, then why aren't they looking at Roxie? Or Charles Whistler?" Joan shook her head slowly. "In fact, they should be looking closer at Charles. You said he was part of the collective, right?"

Priscilla nodded. "I kind of forgot about him. He certainly doesn't seem like an art thief. But you're right. He was the person to discover the Adair. Surely the FBI agents have talked to him." She turned the thought over in her mind for a moment. "But if he's behind it, why didn't he just grab the painting and run? Why let it out of his hands and then put himself in a situation where he'd have to go back and steal it?"

"I have no idea," Joan said, "but I still think he's a good suspect."

Priscilla chewed on her lip as she thought about Joan's comment. The FBI probably already considered Charles a person of interest. Maybe he really did take the painting. But if that were true, why would they let Trudy think Priscilla might be hiding it?

"I'm sure they're checking him out, Joan. I mean, he was the first one to see the Adair. They would have to consider him a possible suspect."

Joan was quiet for a moment. "You know, they're the professionals. I mean, if the FBI can't discover the truth, what chance do we have?"

"I wouldn't go that far," Priscilla said. "We have an advantage over the FBI. We live here. We know people. I think we should keep doing our own investigation. But in the end, I'm confident the professionals will arrive at the right answer."

"Maybe, but sometimes innocent people get charged with crimes, Priscilla. I guess we have to keep digging for the truth. Especially if the FBI thinks you've squirreled the painting away somewhere."

Priscilla smiled at her. "If they tear my cottage apart, they won't find anything. So why should I worry?"

Joan's expression relaxed visibly. "You're right, of course." She paused for a moment before saying, "I certainly would like to know more about Charles. Who was he close to in the collective? What has he been doing? Does he make a good suspect?"

"I didn't mention him to Adrian. I wish I had. Frankly, like I said, I keep forgetting about Charles."

Joan shrugged. "I met him once, before yesterday. He's the kind of person who fades into the background."

"He's connected to the collective and the painting. We need to pay more attention to him, I think." Priscilla shook her head. "We have to find someone who was in the collective who will be candid with us. So far, I get the feeling that everyone is hiding something, but I have no idea what it is."

"I understand what you're saying." Joan tried to wipe off the passenger side window. It was fogging up because of the cold rain. "If someone in the collective took the Adair painting, why did it hang in Marjorie's cottage all those years? Why not eventually take it back?"

Even though they'd already asked themselves this question many times, it was a real sticking point. Something that didn't fit. Before Priscilla came to the island, the cottage sat vacant for months. If someone wanted the painting, it would have been pretty simple to break in and grab it. Yet no one did. Priscilla loved to solve puzzles, but this one was tough. She voiced her concerns out loud to Joan. "As you say, why take the risk to steal a famous painting, hide it, and then abandon it? It simply doesn't make sense, Joan."

"Unless—" Joan started to say.

"The thief died and no one knew the Adair was under Marjorie's painting," Priscilla finished for her. She glanced over at Joan. "We need to find out who died and when."

"So far we know that Billy Manders is gone. Is that it?"

"No," Priscilla said, shaking her head slowly. "My mom and Aunt Marjorie are gone."

"Well, yes, of course, but I don't believe they were involved, Priscilla." Joan frowned at her. "Let's just concentrate on anyone else who's passed away. If they never got the chance to tell anyone, we could find our first thief." She shook her head. "But not our second unless someone has come back from the dead. That thief would have to be someone different."

"But if we can discover how the painting ended up over the mantel in the cottage, we might be able to figure the rest of it out."

"Maybe," Joan said slowly.

Priscilla pulled up in front of her cottage. Trudy's car was already there. When she and Joan got out of the car, Trudy jumped out of hers, a large pink umbrella over her head. Trudy, who was cute, petite, and blonde, could pull it off. If Priscilla bought a pink umbrella, she was convinced she'd look ridiculous.

Joan and Priscilla ran toward the front of the cottage. Priscilla unlocked the door and found Jake waiting for them, his tail wagging. He loved Trudy and Joan and was obviously happy to see them.

As her cousins greeted Jake, Priscilla slipped off her raincoat and held her hands out for their coats. They gave them to her and she hung them up on the coatrack. After everyone wiped her shoes on the large rug in front of the door, Priscilla put the umbrellas on the rug where they could dry off as well.

"Come on in and sit down," she said to Trudy and Joan. "I'll make some coffee and get the sandwiches made before we talk."

"Where's Gail?" Joan asked.

"Couldn't come," Trudy said. "I guess they were overwhelmed with dental emergencies." She rolled her eyes at the last remark.

"There's no need to be snide, Trudy," Joan said sharply. "Gail would be here if she could."

Trudy sighed and plopped down on the couch. Jake followed her and curled up on the floor at her feet. Trudy leaned down and ran her hand over his back. "I know. I'm sorry. I'm just upset. Being questioned by the FBI is very disturbing."

"I know, Trudy," Priscilla said gently. "You two give me a minute, and I'll get us something to eat."

Priscilla hurried into the kitchen. In a few minutes she'd made three chicken salad sandwiches and added a side of red grapes to each plate. She felt bad for Trudy even though they'd all been expecting visits from the FBI. Trudy was a good woman with a big heart, but she also tended to exaggerate things. Surely the FBI hadn't actually told her they believed Priscilla took the Adair painting. What kind of proof did they have? For the first time, Priscilla began to wonder if she might actually be arrested for something she hadn't done. She wanted to call Gerald. Tell him she needed to talk to him. He always made her feel stronger somehow. Always found the right words of encouragement she needed to hear.

But she had to face the truth. Gerald might not be there anymore to help her. She would have to face this trial without him. Facing that reality frightened her.

CHAPTER EIGHTEEN

Priscilla was just getting ready to carry the plates into the living room when Joan joined her. She took the plates, which gave Priscilla time to make some iced tea. When she entered the living room, Joan and Trudy were waiting for her.

"Here's some tea," Priscilla said, handing out glasses. "When we're done, I've got brownies, and I'll make some coffee if you'd like."

Jake stayed where he was, probably hoping someone would accidentally drop some chicken salad on the floor. Priscilla thought about telling him to move away, but his presence seemed to comfort Trudy, so she kept quiet.

After eating a few bites of her sandwich, Trudy put her plate down and turned her attention to Joan and Priscilla. "They knocked on my door about eleven o'clock this morning. I had no idea who it was. I certainly wasn't expecting company." She shook her head slowly. "I was working on plans for the fall festival at church." She glanced back and forth between Joan and Priscilla.

Priscilla got the feeling Trudy wanted them to feel her pain. Trudy, who'd wanted to make it big on Broadway when she was a kid, could be very dramatic when she felt the need.

Priscilla cleared her throat. "I'm sorry you had to go through this, Trudy. I really am. So what kinds of questions did they ask?"

She was trying to be compassionate, but Priscilla wanted the details. Sometimes dealing with Trudy took patience, and Priscilla didn't feel very strong in that virtue today.

Trudy's eyelids fluttered for a moment as she considered Priscilla's question. "They told me who they were and asked if they could come in." She picked up her sandwich and took another bite, slowly chewing it and staring at Joan and Priscilla. Finally she swallowed and put her sandwich down again. "Well, it was something I don't want to experience again." She offered them a shaky smile. Priscilla was just beginning to wonder what would happen if she went over and shook Trudy until the full story tumbled out, when Trudy proceeded. "After they sat down, they asked me what I knew about the painting. I told them the truth. Nothing. I mean, I knew it had been discovered under the other picture, but that was it. I'd never even heard of this Adair guy until this happened." She nodded at Joan. "I told them you knew who he was, but that you're a very talented painter yourself." She offered Joan a beatific smile as if her actions were laudable.

"Trudy," Joan said between gritted teeth, "you basically told them I was a good suspect."

Trudy's eyes widened. "I don't see how…" As realization washed through her expression, Priscilla wanted to laugh—except it really wasn't funny.

"No one will suspect you, Joan," Priscilla said. "Don't worry about it."

"I'm sorry, Joan," Trudy said, her bottom lip quivering. "I think having the FBI in my living room made me so nervous, I just wasn't thinking."

Joan gave her a tight smile. "It's okay, hon. I realize you didn't mean anything by it. We're all on edge. Just tell us what else happened."

Trudy nodded slowly. "They wanted to know if I had any idea who gave the painting to Aunt Marjorie. I told them I didn't. That it had hung above the fireplace ever since I could remember." Trudy bit her lip and stared up at the ceiling for a minute. "They asked why you decided to have the painting cleaned, Priscilla. I thought that was kind of a silly question and told them that. It was dirty. Perfectly understandable." Her eyes lit up as if she'd remembered something else. "Oh, and I asked them why in the world you'd take the painting in to the Art Attack if you knew the Adair was under it. That would make you pretty dumb, wouldn't it?"

"What did they say?" Joan asked.

Trudy wrinkled her nose. "Nothing. They just looked at each other. You know, like they knew something I didn't. I have no idea what they were thinking."

"You said the FBI hinted that Priscilla had the Adair painting," Joan said. "What did they say that led you to believe that?"

"Did I say that?" Trudy frowned, a look of confusion on her face.

Priscilla's earlier thought about shaking her cousin slipped back into her head. With effort, she pushed it away.

"Yes, you did," Joan said. "I'd really like to know why."

"Me too," Priscilla said gently.

Trudy chewed on her lip again. Then her eyes lit up. "Oh, yeah. I remember now." Her expression grew serious. "They asked me questions about the cottage. You know, like how big it was. They knew about the hidden tunnel. Asked if there were any other secret areas. I assumed it was because they think you hid the painting here somewhere."

"So they didn't actually say they thought Priscilla had the painting," Joan said slowly. She turned to gaze at Priscilla. "Still, it doesn't sound good, does it? I think Trudy's conclusion might be right."

"They can search my house if they want to," Priscilla said. "That doesn't worry me. They won't find the painting."

Joan cleared her throat. "I know that, but I still don't like the idea of them going through your things."

Priscilla shrugged. "They have to do what they have to do. I just want the painting to be found."

"Couldn't the thief be some random person?" Trudy asked. "Why do we think it has to be someone we know? I mean, the story about the Adair painting was all over town a couple of hours after it was found. *Anyone* could have taken it. Really."

Priscilla nodded. "You're right, of course, but I still feel there's more to this. Every time I talk to a member of the collective, they act... I don't know, as if there's something they're not telling me. I wish someone would level with me."

"Who have you talked to so far?" Joan asked, taking out a pad of paper and a pen from her purse.

"Let's see..." Priscilla thought for a moment. "Adrian Deering. I don't think he will be very helpful because of his condition. We talked to Tilly..."

"Not for very long," Joan said. "I think we should speak to her again. Tilly has always been an honest, forthright person. We need to sit her down and see if we can find out what everyone is hiding."

"You're probably right," Priscilla said. She nodded toward Trudy. "You talked to Alma, but that wasn't a real conversation."

Trudy sighed. "She's a tough nut. Not sure she'll ever crack. That's if she knows anything at all."

"And there's Mildred," Joan said.

"I might like to talk to her again," Priscilla said. "We've become good friends. Especially after I gave her Hiacoomes." Hiacoomes was a stray cat that used to hang out around Priscilla's cottage. Mildred had lost a cat and gladly took in the stray. They seemed to be very happy together.

"So we need to try to talk to everyone we've spoken to again," Priscilla said with a sigh. "I wish we could pull a Hercule Poirot and call all the suspects together in one room. That might shake out the truth."

"That would be great," Joan said, "but I don't think they'd do it. Not yet anyway." Her eyebrows knit together in a frown. "Who else is on the list?"

"Charles Whistler," Trudy said. "Frankly, I think we should put him at the top of our list. Quite a coincidence that he's the one Roxie called to restore the painting."

"But like we said, he could have simply walked out with the painting and not said a word to anyone," Joan said, a note of frustration in her voice. "He'd have been free and clear. And why uncover the Adair painting if he'd stolen it in the first place?" She shook her head. "I don't think he took it."

Trudy was quiet for a moment. "What about Roxie? Could she have stolen it?"

Joan shrugged. "I don't know, but it's possible. I think we should consider Roxie a suspect too." Joan stopped and wrote something on her notepad. Then she looked up and sighed. "I'm sorry I'm on edge," she said, "but I'm really worried. Especially after someone tried to push Priscilla's car off a cliff." She stared at Priscilla, her face creased with apprehension. "I want you and Jake to come and stay with me until this is over. It's getting too dangerous."

Trudy nodded. "I agree. You're a sitting duck out here."

Priscilla smiled at them, moved by their concern. "Thank you. Really. But I don't feel unsafe. Especially with Jake by my side. If anyone comes near, he'll let me know, and I'll call the police. I promise." It was clear her assurances hadn't changed her cousins' minds. She was getting ready to bolster her comment when someone knocked on her door. "Now what?" she said under her breath. When she opened the door, she found Chief Westin and a couple of his officers standing on her porch. She recognized Officers April Brown and Teddy Holmes. Special Agents Baxter and Peel were a few feet behind them.

The chief looked sheepish. "Priscilla, we need to look through your house. I assured these men that we wouldn't need a search warrant."

Priscilla opened the door wider and stepped aside. "You were right, Chief. I'm very happy to let all of you conduct a thorough search of my house. I have absolutely nothing to hide."

"I appreciate that," the chief said with a backward glance at the stone-faced FBI agents.

Priscilla motioned for them to come inside. Chief Westin asked Priscilla, Trudy, and Joan to stay in the living room while they searched the rest of the cottage. Teddy stood guard in the living room, making sure the three of them stayed put. He looked decidedly uncomfortable. The police searched the living room first, with Baxter and Peel following behind them. Then the group moved toward the back of the house.

"This is just ridiculous," Priscilla whispered to her cousins. She understood why the police had to look for the painting, but why in the world would they think she'd take it home if she'd actually stolen it? "I'd have to be the dumbest criminal in the world to bring that painting into my house."

Trudy, who was sitting next to her, reached over and took her hand. "Hank is a good cop, Priscilla," she said in a low voice. "I know him very well. He's in a difficult situation, and he's doing the best he can. I feel badly for him."

At first, Priscilla bristled at Trudy's words, but after she thought about it for a moment, she realized Trudy was right. The chief *was* in a tough spot, especially with the FBI looking over his shoulder. If she were the chief of police, she'd be doing the same thing. "I'm sorry. You're right. It's just that…" She felt her bottom lip tremble, and she inhaled quickly, trying to hold back her jumbled emotions.

"It's just that you don't like people thinking you're a criminal," Joan finished for her. "I totally understand that. But don't worry. The police won't find anything, and then they'll leave."

Joan had just finished her thought when someone called out the chief's name. Priscilla looked toward the kitchen but she couldn't see who it was. She heard the chief talking to someone. Then there was silence. A few minutes later, he walked into the living room with a strange look on his face.

"Will you stand up, please, Mrs. Grant?" He nodded toward Teddy, who looked shocked. Teddy walked slowly over to where Priscilla sat and helped her to her feet. "Put your hands behind your back please," he said.

Priscilla did as he asked. When she felt the handcuffs going on, she cried out, "What are you doing? What's going on?"

"I'm sorry, Mrs. Grant," Teddy said softly. He looked into her eyes then gave the slightest nod in the direction of the two agents who were conferring with the chief. Priscilla understood. No matter how much Chief Westin trusted her to cooperate, the FBI would expect any arrest to be strictly by the book.

That was when the chief gestured to April, who walked into the room with something in her hands. It was *Seascape in Shadows*. "I'm arresting you for grand larceny, Mrs. Grant," the chief said. He nodded toward Teddy. "Take her down to the station while we finish searching the rest of the house."

CHAPTER NINETEEN

Priscilla knew Joan and Trudy were waiting for her somewhere inside the police station, but for now, she sat in a small room with a table and two chairs, one on each side. She assumed this was where they interrogated suspects. She was on one side of the table, still handcuffed. She had no idea how long she'd been sitting here, but it felt like forever. Thirty minutes? An hour? Even though she wanted to be brave, she couldn't hold back the tears that slipped down her face. Would everyone believe she was a criminal? That she'd stolen the painting? As she continued to wait, Priscilla remembered she'd given the chief an alibi. She was with her cousins at the Inn when the painting was stolen. So why was she here? How could he possibly think she was guilty?

Suddenly, the door opened and Agents Peel and Baxter came in. Agent Peel leaned against the wall and Agent Baxter sat in the chair across from her. He put a file folder on the table, opened it, then stared at it, not saying anything. After several minutes of silence, Priscilla had reached her tipping point. She figured they were trying to break her down, but she had no intention of confessing to something she hadn't done.

"How can you think I stole that painting?" she asked. "I was with my cousins at a local restaurant when it was taken. The chief knows all about it."

Finally, Agent Baxter looked up and met her gaze. "Obviously, you were working with someone else. That person took the painting and then delivered it to you."

Priscilla snorted. "And then, being a great criminal mastermind, I took the painting home and stuck it in my kitchen? Are you serious?"

The agent shrugged. "People believe we won't look certain places. They think they're being clever."

"Well, hiding a valuable stolen painting in my kitchen where it could be found right away isn't clever. It's stupid."

"So you've thought this out?"

Priscilla's mouth dropped open. "What? No, of course not."

"Sounds like it to me."

Priscilla took a deep breath and released it as slowly as she could while counting to ten silently. Losing her temper now wouldn't help anyone. "Look, I only caught a brief glimpse of that painting, but it looked as if it had been completely restored. I don't know how to do that. I'd think a restoration like that would take a lot of time. Have you thought of that?"

Agent Baxter shifted in his chair and looked a little uncomfortable. His partner cleared his throat before saying, "We're having it checked out right now. Hopefully, you didn't damage it."

Priscilla rolled her eyes. "You people are wasting your time. You need to quit bothering me and find out who really took that painting. And why they put it in my house. If they wanted to sell it, why would they put it someplace where you would easily find it? Does that make sense to you?"

Before either agent could answer, the door to the room opened and Chief Westin stepped in. The expression on his face made it clear something was wrong. "I need to speak to you," he said to the two agents, his voice gruff.

"We're a little busy..." Agent Peel started to say.

"Now."

The chief's firm tone got their attention, and the agents followed the chief out of the room. After the door closed, Priscilla could hear their voices, even though she couldn't make out what they were saying. She was certain whoever planted that painting in her kitchen did it the same night someone tried to push her car off the cliff. Jake had tracked them from outside to inside the house. She wished she would have found the painting before the police, but there was no use crying over spilled milk.

She was extremely suspicious about that painting. Why would someone risk so much to steal it and then use it to frame her? Was making her look guilty more important than the money they could have gotten for it on the black market? No one could hate her that much. Something was obviously wrong. She wondered if the painting the police found was a fake. Something the thief was willing to lose. Whatever was going on, she prayed the truth would come out soon. She was cold, tired, and uncomfortable. The chair she sat in was hard, and the handcuffs were chafing her wrists. She was just wondering how much longer she'd have to sit there when the door opened and Chief Westin came in. No sign of Special Agents Baxter and Peel.

The chief didn't say anything, just came over and stood behind her. He reached down and unlocked her handcuffs. Then he walked around to the front of the table.

"You can go," he said, not meeting her eyes.

"Why?" she asked. "What's happened?"

"Special Agent Baxter sent pictures of the painting to their experts. It's a fake. It's not the original copy of *Seascape in Shadows.*"

Although the possibility had occurred to Priscilla she was surprised to hear him confirm her suspicions.

He continued. "We do know the painting we found wasn't recently painted. It's a few decades old. We think the real painting is still out there somewhere. We just don't know where."

"Chief, I think someone tried to set me up. Distract you from finding the real painting."

He nodded. "I'm thinking the same thing." He cleared his throat and finally met her eyes. "I'm sorry, Mrs. Grant. I really am. Someone's playing a dangerous game, and I think we've put you in peril. I want you to know that we'll be patrolling your property regularly, keeping an eye on you, making sure you're safe."

"I appreciate that, Chief," Priscilla said. She stood up, rubbed her wrists, and stretched, trying to loosen her stiff muscles. "No hard feelings. I realize you're just doing your job."

"Thanks, that's kind of you. If you come up with anything that might help us, let me know. The FBI has the case, but we're assisting them. You can contact them or me if something occurs to you that might lead us in the right direction."

"Of course," she said. "I notice the agents aren't in here apologizing. Did they make you do it?"

He shook his head. "No, it was my idea. But they certainly didn't volunteer to tell you they were wrong."

Priscilla smiled, and the chief responded with a quick grin.

"You have some people out here who have been waiting a long time for you," he said. "Why don't you go let them know you're ready to go home."

"I will. Thanks." She walked through the door the chief held open and went down the hall to the lobby. Her cousins were all gathered there, along with Gerald. Although she thought she'd gotten her emotions in check, as soon as she saw their concerned faces, tears welled up in her eyes. Joan rushed over and put her arms around Priscilla.

"Are you okay?" she asked.

"I'm fine," Priscilla choked out. "I don't know why I'm crying. I'm really okay."

"Being arrested is scary," Trudy said. "It's fine to get emotional."

"Are you sure you're okay?" Gerald asked. "They didn't hurt you?"

The chief grunted. "We don't break out the rubber hoses much anymore, Gerald. Of course we didn't hurt her. She's fine."

"She's not fine," Gail snapped. "You arrested an innocent woman. You handcuffed her and frightened her, and you scared her family and friends. Shame on you."

Priscilla disengaged herself from Joan's embrace. "Don't say that, Gail," she said, wiping her damp face with her hand. "The chief was only doing his job. The person to blame is whoever planted that fake picture in my house."

"Fake?" Gerald said. "So it's not the original Adair?"

"No, but the chief said it was old. Not recently painted."

Joan frowned. "I don't understand."

"I don't either," Priscilla said. "There's a lot more going on here than what I originally thought." She sighed. "But right now, I just want to go home. Will someone give me a ride please?"

Before anyone else could speak up, Gerald took her arm. "I'll see you home, Priscilla."

Although she wasn't sure she was in the mood to be near Gerald right now, she was too upset to argue. She just nodded.

"We'll call you later," Gail said. "You get some rest."

Trudy gave her a quick hug. "We love you, Priscilla."

Another wave of emotion washed over her. "I know," she said, her voice breaking. "I love you too."

She'd just turned toward Gerald when Agent Baxter stepped into the lobby. "I need to remind you not to leave the area, Mrs. Grant," he said solemnly.

"Haven't you threatened her enough?" Joan snapped. "Why don't you spend your time looking for the real thief and leave my cousin alone?"

He scowled at her. "We're looking at several possibilities, but it's important that Mrs. Grant understands she's still a person of interest."

Joan started to respond, but Priscilla hushed her. "No more, Joan. Please. I'm too tired to argue with him or you or anyone else today. I just want to go home."

Although everyone fell silent, the warning issued by the grim FBI agent hung over Priscilla like a thick, heavy blanket.

CHAPTER TWENTY

Priscilla was quiet as Gerald drove her home. He seemed to understand that she needed the silence to think...and to regroup. Being arrested was something she'd never anticipated. She didn't want to tell Rachel about it, but she realized she'd have to at some point. Before someone else told her. Why did she feel so guilty? She hadn't done anything wrong, but now she felt like a criminal. It wasn't a good feeling.

"I want to take you to supper tomorrow night," Gerald said softly, breaking the silence. "Please don't say no. I want to get you out for a while. Give you a break from all this. Besides, I think we need to talk."

"About what?" Priscilla asked.

"We need to talk about the possibility of my moving to Boston."

She shrugged. "It's your life, Gerald. Besides, I totally understand why you'd want to be near your family."

He paused for several seconds. "Let's leave it there for now, okay? You've been through enough for one day. We'll talk about this tomorrow night. I'll pick you up at seven."

She just nodded. She was too tired to argue. All she wanted was to go home, make a cup of tea, sit in front of the fire, and fall asleep on the couch with Jake curled up at her feet. It sounded like heaven. First though, she needed to take a shower. As strange as it sounded, she felt dirty. She wanted to put on other clothes. Clothes that hadn't been worn by someone under arrest. She knew she was being overly dramatic, but it was how she felt.

A few minutes later, Gerald pulled up in front of her cottage. "Let me come in with you. In case the police left the place in a mess. You rest, and I'll clean up."

"I appreciate that, Gerald, but I just want to be alone. If the police tossed my house, I'll deal with it."

"Are you sure?"

She nodded. "I need some time to myself. I'll see you tomorrow night."

"Okay. Priscilla?"

"Yeah?"

"You didn't deserve to be treated like this. I know you had nothing to do with the theft of that painting. I assume you know that, but I want to say it. To make sure you know that I would never suspect you of anything illegal. You're the most honest, trustworthy person I've ever met."

Although his words of comfort seemed a little sappy, she smiled. "Thank you. It really does help to hear someone say that. For some strange reason I feel as if I've done something wrong."

"Don't let what happened get into your head. You're completely innocent."

"I know that here." She pointed to her heart. "But there's a voice up here"—she tapped her forehead with her index finger—"that keeps whispering things that make me feel awful. Like I need to hide from people."

"You know whose voice that is," Gerald said gently. "Don't listen to him. Listen to the voice in your heart. That's where God will speak to you."

Priscilla felt her eyes well up. "You're right. Thanks."

She started to open the car door when another car pulled up next to them. Joan. And she had Jake with her. Priscilla had been worried about Jake. Wondered where he was and who was taking care of him. She was so relieved to see him.

She said goodbye to Gerald and got out of the car. At the same time, Joan opened her car door. Jake jumped over her and ran straight to Priscilla.

"Oh, Jake," Priscilla said, bending down and putting her arms around him. "I'm so glad to see you."

"He missed you too," Joan said, walking up next to them. She waved at Gerald, who waved back and then put his car in gear. As he drove away, Joan said, "Let's get you both inside. It's stopped raining for a while, but it's supposed to start up again before long."

The gray skies echoed the way Priscilla felt inside. When they walked into her cottage, she was surprised to find it in fairly good shape. She was afraid it would be a disaster, with her belongings spread out all over the place. Maybe that only happened in TV cop shows. An attempt to straighten up had been made, but Priscilla immediately saw things out of place.

"You sit down," Joan said. "I'm going to make you a cup of tea and straighten up."

Priscilla started to repeat what she'd said to Gerald, but Joan hushed her. "You won't know I'm here. I won't talk to you. I just want to put your house back together so you don't feel violated. And I won't take no for an answer."

Once again, Priscilla's emotions expressed themselves in tears. She took off her coat and sat down, unable to respond to Joan's act of kindness. Joan put her hand on Priscilla's shoulder and patted her softly.

"Everything will be all right. I promise. Okay?"

Priscilla nodded. A few seconds later, Joan withdrew her hand and went into the kitchen. Priscilla could hear her filling the tea kettle and moving things around, probably putting everything back where it belonged. Priscilla pulled her legs up and covered herself with the quilt she kept on the arm of the couch. Jake immediately jumped up and positioned himself next to her. He laid his head on her leg and looked up at her with his big brown eyes. That was the last thing she remembered until she woke up. The house was quiet. Joan sat in a chair near the couch, reading a book.

"Hey, sleepyhead," she said.

"I can't believe I actually fell asleep," Priscilla said. She slowly pulled her legs from underneath Jake, who looked up at her with concern. She sat up straight and put her hand on his head. He scooted up closer to her.

"I've got some supper warming in the oven," Joan said. "I'll make you that cup of tea, and then I'll get out of here so you can relax on your own."

"Stay and eat with me," Priscilla said. "Really. You don't need to rush off."

"I thought you wanted to spend some time alone."

Priscilla smiled at her. "I couldn't face Gerald right now, but having you around doesn't bother me. I feel relaxed around you."

"Well, I'll eat a little bit with you, but then I'll probably take off. I want you to have a peaceful evening. And I need to get home to Sister."

Before Priscilla could respond, her phone rang. She reached over and picked it up. After answering there was a moment of silence. Then she heard, "Priscilla? This is Tilly Snyder. I...Well, we...We need to talk to you. Me and Mildred. And Alma Whitaker. We heard what happened today, and we think it's awful. There are some things you need to know. Could you meet with us this evening for a little while?"

Priscilla was surprised by Tilly's request, but also intrigued. "I—I guess I could do that," she said. "Could you possibly come here?"

She could hear Tilly put her hand over the receiver and say something to someone else. A moment later, she said, "I guess that would be okay. Would seven o'clock work for you?"

Priscilla glanced at the clock. She actually had no idea what time it was. A little before six. "Yes, that would be fine. I look forward to seeing you." She hung up the phone and shook her head. "You won't believe this. That was Tilly. She wants to talk to me. She's bringing Alma and Mildred with her."

Joan's mouth dropped open. "Mildred and Alma together? In one room? Wow." She frowned at Priscilla. "What do they want?"

Priscilla shrugged. "They have something to tell me. Something they feel I need to know. Tilly said she heard what happened today."

"Let's get some food into you," Joan said. "Then I'll skedaddle before they get here."

"I wish you wouldn't," Priscilla said. "I'd feel better if you were here. I might need a witness."

Joan laughed. "I was hoping you'd ask me to stay. I must admit I'm curious. What I'll do is dish you up some supper and then make a quick trip to my house to get Sister. Jake will appreciate the company while we visit with the women." She got up and hurried into the kitchen where Priscilla and Jake joined her. Joan had something simmering on the stove. The kitchen was spotless, everything in its place. Priscilla was touched to see how hard Joan had worked to put her house back to normal.

As she waited for supper, she wondered what was so important that Tilly, Mildred, and Alma had banded together. Since Mildred and Alma tried to avoid each other as much as possible, whatever they had to say must be significant. Would their visit finally bring some resolution to the questions that so desperately needed to be answered?

CHAPTER TWENTY-ONE

Priscilla had finished supper, and Joan and Sister had just returned when someone knocked on the front door.

"You go on in there," Joan said. "I'll clean up."

"Please come with me," Priscilla pleaded. "I don't feel like facing this alone."

"Are you sure? They may not want me listening in."

"I don't care what they want," Priscilla snapped. "I'm getting a little tired of being used by whoever is behind the theft of that painting."

"Whoa, cousin," Joan said with a smile. "I've got your back." The doorbell rang, and Jake started barking. "We need to let them in. It's raining."

"Okay," Priscilla said, "then let's do this. Together."

Joan picked up the pot of chili she'd made for supper and transferred it to the fridge. "Don't let me forget to put this in a proper container before I go home."

"Deal," Priscilla said with a grateful smile. "And thanks."

They left the kitchen and headed to the front door. On the way, Priscilla grabbed Jake and Sister and put them in the bedroom so they wouldn't disrupt the meeting. They were perfectly happy just to be together and didn't object at all when she pulled the door closed and joined Joan in the living room where she stood waiting.

Before Priscilla opened the front door she reached up and smoothed her hair, praying under her breath. It was time for answers. Being arrested had made her more determined than ever to uncover the truth about *Seascape in Shadows*.

When she swung the door open, she found Tilly standing there, Alma and Mildred behind her.

"Come in," Priscilla said. She stood to the side and waved the women inside. She noticed that all of them looked a little skittish—as if they would rather be anywhere but here.

Alma spotted Joan standing in the living room, next to the couch. "What's she doing here?" she asked. "We want to talk to you alone, Priscilla. This isn't for anyone else's ears."

"Then I'll have to say good night and ask you to leave," Priscilla answered. "If what you have to tell me can't be said in front of my cousin, then you should go home."

Alma's eyebrows arched, making her hawk-like features even more intimidating. She started to say something, but Tilly grabbed her by the arm and told her to hush.

"It's fine if Joan stays," Tilly said. "It's time the truth came out. I'm sorry we kept things from you, Priscilla. We honestly didn't think we knew anything that could help you—until you were arrested. We realized that it was possible our secrets were hurting people." She let go of Alma, who didn't look too happy about the turn of events but kept her mouth closed. However, her lips were shaped into a thin line of disapproval.

"Please sit down," Priscilla said. "Would anyone like a cup of coffee?"

All three women accepted, and Joan went to the kitchen to get the coffee and some shortbread cookies Priscilla had baked a few days earlier. Once everyone was ready, Tilly, who was apparently the spokesperson for the group, took a deep breath and trained her gaze on Priscilla.

"Fifty years ago, we were part of the Tisbury Collective. The collective was made up of the three of us, your aunt Marjorie, your mother, Billy Manders, Raymond Hill, Dora Metcalf, Charles Whistler, and our teacher, Adrian Deering."

"Are you aware that Adrian is in Harbor's Rest Nursing Home?" Priscilla asked, staring right at Mildred.

The look of surprise on Mildred's face made it obvious she hadn't known. But Tilly nodded. "Yes, I know he's there."

"He thinks his friends have deserted him," Joan said. "Why don't you visit him?"

The three women exchanged looks, and Tilly cleared her throat. "Let me finish telling you what we came here to say. Maybe that will help answer your question."

"All right. Go ahead."

Tilly picked up her coffee cup and took a sip. Priscilla glanced at Joan, who looked back at her with a raised eyebrow. It was obvious she thought this visit was odd.

Finally, Tilly said, "Billy Manders passed away ten years ago. When he died, we all thought the past was behind us. But finding the Adair painting brought it all back. We never thought that painting would ever show up."

"You're getting ahead of yourself," Mildred said. "Go back and tell her the story from the beginning."

Tilly nodded. "You're right. Thank you." She took a deep breath and said, "Before I do that, you should know that Raymond Hill recently passed away as well. As far as we know, Dora is still alive. The last I heard she was in Wyoming, but that was a long time ago. She might not be there now. Does anyone know where Dora lives now?" She looked at the other two women. Alma shook her head, but Mildred didn't. "Mildred, do you know where she is?"

"Believe it or not, she recently moved back to Vineyard Haven. Her health isn't good. She moved in with her daughter, Cicely. I happened to run into Cicely about a month ago, and she told me about her mother."

"Why didn't you tell us?" Alma asked, her voice sharp and accusatory.

Mildred shrugged. "Why should I? None of us were close to her."

"That's not true," Tilly said. "Dora and I were friends."

Mildred scowled at her. "If you were such good friends, why didn't you stay in touch with her?"

Alma and Tilly were both silent after Mildred's question.

Priscilla couldn't help but wonder what had happened between the old friends that had caused such a split. And what did it have to do with *Seascape in Shadows*?

"I really don't see where this is going," she said.

"I'm sorry," Tilly said. "I'm just trying to keep things in order so you'll understand what happened that summer." She rubbed her hands together as if they were cold. "As you know, we only met in the summer, when Adrian was free from his teaching duties at the college." She smiled at Priscilla. "Your mother would attend as well. She and Marjorie got along well back then, although there was some tension between them. Marjorie had a big crush on Billy, but he wasn't interested. Your mother was Billy's best friend. There was never anything romantic between them, but Marjorie would never believe that." She leaned back on the couch and folded her arms across her chest. "I'll tell you the real reason your mother and Marjorie had a falling-out that summer. It was over Billy, but there's more to it than you know."

"This is interesting, but what does it have to do with the stolen Adair painting?" Joan asked, echoing the same thing Priscilla was thinking.

"It has everything to do with it." Tilly leaned forward and picked up her coffee cup. She didn't take a drink, she just stared into it. "The first thing you need to know is that during that last summer, Adrian gave us all an assignment. It was to be completed before the class ended. He told us to pick a famous painting and make a copy of it. Copying other painters is a good way to learn technique. We all picked an artist and a painting we admired."

"Did someone paint *Seascape in Shadows*?" Priscilla asked. "Is that where the fake copy came from?"

"Yes. Billy Manders. And he did a masterful job. It was beautiful. Frankly, I couldn't see any difference between the Adair and Billy's painting. I fell in love with it. Asked Billy if I could buy it from him, but he said no. That's when I got the print that hangs in my home." Tilly drank the last of her coffee and held the cup out. "Could I have some more?"

Although she was getting rather impatient, Priscilla nodded. She started to take Tilly's cup when Joan reached over and grabbed it first.

"I've got it," she said. "You all go ahead."

"Thank you, Joan," Priscilla said gratefully, glad she'd asked her to stay.

As Joan left the room, Tilly continued. "Not long after that, *Seascape in Shadows*, the real one, arrived in Plymouth. Part of a traveling exhibition. Billy was so excited. Although we all wanted to go, in the end, just Billy, Raymond, and Adrian went. Billy had a friend who worked for the museum where *Seascape* was going to be exhibited. He told Billy he'd let them in to see it before it went on exhibit. It was a chance to see the painting up close. They were all very excited about the prospect."

"Why didn't the rest of you go?" Priscilla asked.

"We all wanted to," Tilly said. "But with Marjorie's accusations about Billy, your mother didn't feel it would help the situation by going on an overnight trip with him. She also didn't feel she could leave you and your dad behind, and he wasn't interested in seeing the painting." She waved her hand toward Alma and Mildred. "We had to work. We all had jobs, including Marjorie and Dora."

"Okay, so Raymond, Billy, and Adrian went to the exhibit. Then what?"

Tilly looked at Mildred who nodded. Tilly stared down at her hands for a few seconds and then said, "After they left, the rest of us got together as usual, even though Adrian was gone. We noticed right away that Billy's painting was missing. We just figured he took it home to work on it some more."

Priscilla frowned at her. "Did he?"

Tilly wrapped her arms around her knees and began to rock back and forth. "It wasn't until we heard the Adair was missing that we suspected he took the painting with him to Plymouth so he could exchange it for the original when he stole it from the exhibit."

CHAPTER TWENTY-TWO

The room became so silent, Priscilla could hear people breathing. She couldn't believe what she'd just heard. "Are you saying Billy stole *Seascape in Shadows*?" This didn't square with what she'd heard about Billy Manders. She couldn't see her mother and her aunt having feelings for someone so dishonest.

Tilly nodded. "What else are we to think? How big a coincidence would it be if Billy just happened to choose that painting to copy at the same time it was coming to Plymouth?"

"So Raymond and Adrian didn't know anything about his plans?" Priscilla asked.

"Look, this is all conjecture. We have no proof. If we'd been sure, we would have contacted the authorities. We don't think Raymond or Adrian were involved, but we could be wrong."

"But I don't get it," Joan jumped in. "If Billy's copy was exchanged for the real painting, why is it here—assuming, of course, that the one found in Priscilla's kitchen is Billy's?"

"We think something went wrong," Mildred said. "It's just a guess, but I believe that before Billy and his pal could switch the painting, the theft was discovered. Billy came home with the real painting, along with his copy."

"That's quite an assumption," Priscilla said.

"It's the only thing that makes sense," Tilly said. "Maybe it didn't happen exactly that way, but it was obvious something happened to Billy's original plan."

"And the museum had no idea that one of its employees conspired with Billy to steal the painting?" Priscilla asked.

Mildred shook her head. "No. He was never charged with anything. We think he decided to keep his mouth shut about the plan. That way he kept his job—and he didn't spend years in prison for attempted theft. Of course, Billy might have simply threatened him. Told him to keep quiet or he'd blame the whole thing on him."

"We can't prove that either, but we're pretty sure that's what happened. Billy and Raymond were friends when they left town and went to Plymouth. When they returned, they weren't speaking. Raymond was never the same after that, and he left town soon afterward. We think he and Billy must have had a huge fight about what Billy did. We think Raymond just couldn't bring himself to turn in a friend."

"But you're not really sure about any of this, are you?" Priscilla asked.

"No," Tilly said. "Billy would only talk to Charlotte about what happened. And she didn't share anything with us. I think she was trying to protect us. We couldn't be charged as accessories if we didn't know the truth." She sighed. "We've thought about this for fifty years, Priscilla, and even though we're guessing about a lot of it, our conclusions are the only ones that make sense."

Mildred cleared her throat. "I overheard a conversation between Charlotte and Billy once. Billy said something about going to jail if he told the truth about *it*. I told Tilly and Alma about it. Of course, we can't be sure they were talking about the Adair. But I think they were. That's one of the reasons we believe we're right about what happened."

"We asked Charlotte many times to tell us what she knew," Alma said. "She would just smile sadly and tell us to pray for Billy. Even though we weren't sure about all the facts, we were certain Billy must be guilty." She exchanged looks with Tilly and Mildred. "It might sound wrong, but we decided between us that we would let things play out. We didn't want to make the police suspicious of Billy or blacken his name if he was innocent."

"And then . . . " Tilly said. "Right before Raymond left town . . . "

"He was angry," Mildred said. "Really angry. He accused Billy of stealing right in front of the group. He didn't say what it was he thought Billy took, but we had to wonder if he wasn't talking about the painting."

"So he did take it?" Priscilla asked. "But then how did the Adair turn up in my living room? Underneath the painting of my cottage and my lighthouse?" Priscilla was trying to follow Tilly's story, but she found it more confusing than helpful.

"We had no idea that's what happened to the painting," Tilly said solemnly, "although now it makes perfect sense. We should have realized . . . " She looked at Mildred and Alma. They both nodded.

"Tell me," Priscilla said simply, although she was fairly certain she knew what Tilly was getting ready to say.

Tilly cleared her throat again. "We believe either Billy or your mother painted over the Adair. Marjorie said that someone had dropped off the painting at her house with a letter telling her it was a gift from a secret admirer. Priscilla, who else could that have been except your mother? She knew your aunt would cherish the painting and take good care of it. She was right for fifty years."

"Actually, she was right even after that," Mildred said to Tilly. "Priscilla took it to be cleaned because she wanted to keep the painting in good shape."

"But again, this is only what we've guessed," Tilly said. "None of us know for sure that it was your mother who took the painting from Billy and gave it to Marjorie. Frankly, if we'd known, I don't know what we would have done. It certainly would have presented us with a moral dilemma. Maybe your mother knew that, and it's why she never told anyone."

Priscilla nodded. "So after all these years Charles uncovers the Adair, and here we are." Priscilla was surprised that her mother would take a chance like that. Hiding a stolen painting? It had to be illegal. How could she have done such a thing?

As if she could read Priscilla's mind, Tilly said, "Your mom cared deeply for Billy. Like a brother. I don't know exactly why Billy didn't leave town with the painting. Maybe he thought we knew what he'd done. Or maybe he realized he wasn't going to be able to sell it after all."

"Are you absolutely certain Adrian wasn't involved?" Joan asked.

Tilly shrugged. "We can't guarantee that he didn't know anything, but I can't imagine Billy telling him. Adrian loves art. If he thought for one moment that the stolen Adair was nearby—that it could be recovered—I'm convinced he would have told the authorities. Of course, I can't prove that. I can only say that we never saw any indication that he knew about the theft. After Raymond left, the group wasn't the same. Not long after an uh...incident between your mother and Marjorie, we broke up. We never talked about the missing painting after that. I think we all just wanted to forget about it."

"What incident?" Priscilla asked. "What happened between my mom and Marjorie?"

Tilly took a deep breath. "I told you I'd share the real reason your mother and your aunt quarreled that last summer. Here it is." She leaned forward. "Your mother and Billy spent so much time together after he got back from Plymouth, your aunt became convinced they were having an affair. She was really angry with Charlotte. She even threatened to tell your father that Charlotte was cheating on him with Billy. Of course, she wasn't. Charlotte couldn't tell Marjorie the truth. Couldn't tell her about the painting."

"Which was hanging over Marjorie's fireplace," Mildred said. "Your mother risked her relationship with her sister to protect Billy. Right or wrong, she did what she felt she had to do."

"She must have really cared for him," Joan said softly.

Tilly nodded. "She did. He loved her too."

"But didn't she actually put Aunt Marjorie at risk?" Joan asked. "I mean, if the original had been found..."

"I honestly don't believe she thought it would ever be uncovered. In Charlotte's mind, the painting was safe, Billy hadn't profited from his theft, and he was safe. Was there another way?"

Tilly shrugged. "I don't know. But I do suspect Charlotte truly believed this was the only way to protect everyone. Believe it or not, I think giving it to Marjorie was a way of saying how much she actually trusted her sister. She knew the painting would be safe with her."

Priscilla leaned back in her chair. At least now she had some idea of how the Adair painting ended up over her fireplace. She wasn't sure how she felt about her mother covering up for a thief. *Someone* had painted over it who was close to Billy Manders, if he didn't do it himself. Was it her mother? Surely there was more to the story. But for now, this would have to be enough for her.

As she turned this information over in her mind, something jumped out. "What concerns me now is that if Billy had the copy, and he's dead, how did it show up here? Who brought it to Tisbury?"

Tilly shook her head. "We have absolutely no idea, but it worries us too. When we heard it had been used to frame you, we knew we had to talk to you. We can't tell you who's behind this, but at least you have the backstory. I hope it helps you." She stood up. "We've told you everything we possibly can. I realize you will have to share this story with the authorities. We're prepared to talk to them. Frankly, I don't believe they can charge us with anything. We were never able to confirm our suspicions. And that's all they are. Suspicions. And as far as the recent theft of the real painting, we don't have a clue who took it."

"But we know it wasn't Billy," Alma said. "He's been gone almost ten years."

"If the police or the FBI want to talk to me, I'll be happy to sit down with them," Tilly said. "I hope they'll leave you alone after they hear our story."

Priscilla stood up and faced Tilly. "Thank you for telling me the truth," she said. She smiled at Mildred and Alma. "My thanks to you too. I know it took courage to say something. You could have kept quiet and stayed out of it."

"We weren't happy keeping these secrets," Mildred said. "We just didn't want to hurt you or your mother. She was a good friend. The kind of person who would shield her friends from harm."

"Looks like Billy got away with the original theft," Priscilla said. "But at least he never got the chance to sell the Adair. That's something."

"Yes, it's a big something." Tilly smiled. "He never made a penny off his dirty deed. That makes me feel pretty good."

"We've been to see Adrian," Priscilla said. "We hoped he might be able to tell us something, but I can see that's a lost cause.

"He might have suspected something since he was with Billy and Raymond in Plymouth," Tilly said, "but I doubt we'll ever know. Not with the shape he's in now."

"What are you talking about?" Mildred said. "Is something wrong with him?"

Tilly nodded. "He was moved to Harbor's Rest Nursing Home, Mildred. After his wife died, he became...confused. He needs care beyond what his family could give him."

The look on Mildred's face surprised Priscilla. She was even more shocked to see tears in her eyes. It was obvious Mildred cared about Adrian. She certainly wasn't a touchy-feely type of person. At least now Priscilla knew Mildred hadn't known that Adrian was in the nursing home. "I—I haven't kept in touch with him," Mildred said. She gave Priscilla a sad smile. "I had a crush on Adrian Deering when I was younger, but my feelings weren't returned. There was a big difference in our ages."

"Back then the difference was important," Tilly said softly. "Not that important anymore."

Mildred sniffed and shook her head. "Thank you, Tilly, but I have no interest in Mr. Deering anymore." She straightened her back, and the corners of her mouth turned down. This was the Mildred Priscilla knew. Tough, proud, and unemotional. She and Alma were like oil and water. Getting a glimpse of the past and of a softer, gentler Mildred had certainly been an experience. However, it was pretty clear things were going back to normal now.

"I'm not sure about sharing this with the FBI," Priscilla said. "None of you have any proof that what you suspect actually took place. Is there anyone still alive who knows for certain what happened?"

Tilly nodded. "Only one that I know of. Dora Metcalf. She was really close to your mom. We were friends too, but we didn't have the kind of relationship she and Charlotte had. If Charlotte unburdened herself to anyone besides Billy, it would have been Dora."

Priscilla wanted to talk to Dora. Find out what she knew. But she didn't want to direct the FBI to a sick, frail old woman who was probably living out the last days of her life with her family. Besides, did Priscilla want to know for certain who painted over the Adair? What if Dora confirmed that one of the culprits was her mother? Could she accept the knowledge that her mother was responsible for hiding a valuable and beloved painting from its rightful owners for all these years?

CHAPTER TWENTY-THREE

Priscilla and Joan sat in the living room quietly contemplating the information Tilly, Mildred, and Alma had just shared.

"Well, that was interesting," Joan said finally.

Priscilla nodded. "They may have it exactly right, but the authorities aren't going to be interested in what anyone thinks happened. They want facts."

"Well, you know from Adrian that your mother sketched the cottage and the lighthouse. Maybe if you could find those sketches..."

"It would prove she drew them. Not that she did the painting."

"But what if the sketches were exactly like the painting?"

Priscilla considered this for a moment. "That might help. But it also means I implicate my mother in the theft of the Adair painting."

"She didn't steal it," Joan said.

"Yeah, she just hid a valuable stolen painting from the people who own it. I doubt the museum would appreciate that."

Joan sighed. "You're right. Would that make her an accessory to the theft?"

"I have no idea," Priscilla said. "There's really not a way to put a positive spin on it."

"I think your mother's loyalty to her friend is admirable," Joan said. "I always liked her, but now...She's more real to me."

Priscilla felt her throat tighten. "Yeah, me too," she said in a choked voice. It was true. Her mother had gone above and beyond to protect someone she loved, even though she placed herself in a precarious position. Priscilla missed her mother and wished she could talk to her about Billy and the painting. But that conversation would have to wait for heaven.

"So now what?" Joan asked.

Priscilla held up a note Tilly had written and given to her before she left. "I talk to Dora Metcalf. Her last name is Genner now. Tilly gave me her daughter's name. Cicely Howard. She didn't know her address, but it shouldn't be too hard to find."

"Do you think she'll actually tell you anything?"

Priscilla stifled a yawn. It had been a long day. "I have no idea, but this seems to be our last chance to find the truth."

"It's still possible that Adrian knows something."

"Yes, but I don't think the authorities will take the word of someone suffering from memory loss. I'll probably talk to him again, but just for my own information. The poor man has been through enough."

Joan held her arms out and stretched. "Well, Cousin, I'd better get home—unless you'd like me to stay."

Priscilla shook her head. "I'm sure I'll be fine. You go on home and get some sleep. I'll talk to you in the morning." She reached over and took Joan's hand. "Thank you. I don't know what I'd do without you."

"You'd be fine, but I'm glad to do whatever I can to help. If you need anything tonight, just call. I'll come back."

Priscilla let go of her hand. "I know you would, but I'm so beat I'll probably be asleep as soon as my head hits the pillow."

"Okay." As Joan stood up, she pointed toward the bedroom door. "I'll try to pry the two buddies apart. Does Jake need to go out?"

"Yeah. I'll walk him before I go to bed."

Joan frowned at her. "I'm glad you feel safe, but I'm still concerned, Priscilla. We can't forget that someone tried to push you over the cliff."

"You know, I'm not even sure about that now," Priscilla said. "Maybe it was just someone who was trying to tell me something. You know, like I had a taillight out or something. Then maybe their foot slipped off the brake."

Joan stared at Priscilla with her mouth open and her eyes wide. "Are you kidding me?" she said after a brief pause. "Priscilla, you need to take threats seriously. That settles it. Sister and I are going with you two. We'll leave after you're both back inside with the doors locked."

Priscilla started to argue, but Joan waved her protestations away with her hand. "No. No, I won't listen. We're going with you, and that's that."

Although Joan's attitude could have irritated Priscilla a little bit, the determined look on her face made Priscilla laugh. "Okay. I know when I'm beat. You're as stubborn as . . ."

"You are?" Joan finished for her.

"I was going to say a mule, but your suggestion might be more accurate."

The women shared a laugh as they fetched their coats, let the dogs out of the bedroom and headed for the front door.

"Wait a minute," Priscilla said. "I need to get my keys. After the other night, I've started locking my front door."

"What happened the other night?" Joan asked, as she fastened Sister's leash to her collar.

Priscilla told her about Jake tracking someone outside the house. "I think that's when the fake painting was planted. That was enough to convince me to lock the door when I take Jake out."

"Priscilla!" Joan said. "That's even more of a reason for you not to stay out here alone. That settles it. I'm staying the night."

Priscilla started to say something, but Joan cut her off. "I don't want to hear it. I'm staying. That's it."

Priscilla laughed. "I was going to say that if you wanted to stay, it would make me feel better."

Joan chuckled. "Well, finally. I won, and I didn't even have to argue with you."

"I was fine until I started telling you about Jake tracking someone. It really does make me a little nervous."

"Let's take these two for a walk," Joan said, "and then we'll come back and settle in for the night."

When they stepped outside, they found the rain had finally stopped. The night was chilly, and the moon peeked out from between clouds racing across the sky. Priscilla found herself looking around, making sure they were alone.

Both dogs seemed eager to finish their walk and get back to the house, so it wasn't long before they found themselves heading back. As they neared the cottage, from down the road, headlights from a car flashed on and the car drove slowly toward them. Priscilla tightened her grasp on Jake's leash, but whoever drove the car didn't seem to be aggressive. As it neared, she realized it was a police cruiser. By the time they reached the cottage, the car had parked. The driver's side door opened, and the front porch light illuminated a large figure. Chief Westin walked over to where the two women stood waiting.

"Good evening, Mrs. Grant," he said as he approached. "I wanted you to know that we're keeping an eye on you."

"Really, Chief?" Priscilla said angrily. "When will you believe I had nothing to do with the theft of that painting?"

"I think that's what he's trying to tell you, Priscilla," Joan said gently.

The chief nodded. "I'm not watching your property because I suspect you," he said. "I'm watching out for you because I believe someone really did try to force you off the cliff the other night. I also believe the same person planted that painting in your kitchen." He took off his hat and held it in his hands. "I had to suspect you, Mrs. Grant. It's my job to look at the circumstances and try to find the truth. But I'm certain now you're a victim in this situation. I'm sorry it's been so hard for you."

The sense of relief that washed over Priscilla was so strong it made her feel a little weak in the knees. When she stumbled, Joan reached out and grabbed her arm.

"Why don't we go inside?" Joan said. "We actually have some things to tell you, I think. Or do we, Priscilla?"

"We do, Chief," Priscilla said. "Unfortunately, it isn't the proof you need. But what we've learned might at least point you in the right direction."

"That would be great," the chief said. "I'm willing to listen to whatever you have to tell me. The FBI is riding this thing pretty hard. It's their case, but they expect our assistance. We haven't been able to give them much help."

"Not sure what we tell you will change anything," Priscilla said, "but at least we can give you some background information. I hope it will help you in some way."

"I have something to tell you too," he said. "Charles Whistler has disappeared."

Priscilla's mouth fell open. "Disappeared? What do you mean?"

"He's left town, and no one seems to know where he is." The chief frowned. "Looks a little suspicious, doesn't it?"

"Yes, it does." Although Priscilla had been looking forward to a good night's sleep, knowing the chief no longer considered her a suspect gave her a renewed sense of determination. She desperately wanted to find the person who'd taken the painting. Could it have been Charles? Where was he? As she went inside with Joan and Chief Westin, she prayed they'd find the thief before he left town. Leaving this mystery unsolved didn't sit well with her. Priscilla's mother and her aunt had become part of the story. Now it was personal.

CHAPTER TWENTY-FOUR

Joan ordered Priscilla to sit down and rest while she fetched coffee for the chief. Priscilla decided on a cup of decaf tea. After getting herself a cup of coffee, Joan sat down on the couch next to Priscilla.

"So tell me what you've discovered," the chief said after taking a sip from his cup.

First Priscilla told him about the Tisbury Collective. "Adrian Deering, a teacher at the local college, led the group. They only met in the summer because of his job with the school."

"Does he still live in the area?" the chief asked.

"Yes, he recently moved into the Harbor's Rest Nursing Home. He... Well, he's suffering from a debilitating condition. Memory loss. Happened after his wife died."

The chief nodded. "Go on," he said.

"Adrian gave his students an assignment," she said. "Copy a famous painting. One of his students, Billy Manders, chose *Seascape in Shadows*. This was before it was stolen from the museum in Plymouth."

The chief's eyebrows arched. "Is that the painting we found?"

Priscilla nodded. "We think it must be. From here on out, all we can tell you is conjecture."

"Yours?"

"No," Priscilla said slowly. "This comes from other students in the group. None of the people I talked to were involved in the theft of the Adair painting. If they had known who took it, they would have come forward. However, secrets were well kept. So from here on out..."

"You're telling me what might have happened but nothing we can use to arrest a suspect."

Priscilla nodded. "Exactly."

He sighed. "All right. I guess at this point I'll take whatever I can get."

Priscilla slowly and carefully went through the story. Except for a few details she'd decided to keep to herself, she told him everything. When she finished, she looked at Joan. "Did I forget anything?"

Joan slowly shook her head. Priscilla was certain her cousin knew she'd purposely kept some information from the chief, but Joan didn't say anything. Priscilla hadn't mentioned Dora Metcalf. Before the police and the FBI showed up at her daughter's house, Priscilla wanted to talk to Dora and see if she actually knew anything that might help. Frightening a frail elderly woman for no good reason was something Priscilla wanted to avoid if at all possible.

Chief Westin listened very carefully to Priscilla. "Are you going to tell me who shared this with you?" he asked when she finished.

"Do I have to?"

The chief was quiet for a moment. Then he said, "Not yet, but at some point we may need those names."

"The people involved have no problem with that," Priscilla said. "If it helps you find the thief."

"I'm not sure it does," he said. "I want to know who brought the copy of *Seascape in Shadows* back to Tisbury. That's the person we're looking for." He cocked his head and peered at Priscilla through his bushy eyebrows. "Any idea who that might be?"

Priscilla shook her head. "Not a clue. We think Billy Manders took the painting with him when he left. But he died ten years ago. No one knows who could have acquired it."

"Might be good to look at recent visitors to Tisbury," Joan said. "Check the hotels and bed-and-breakfasts."

"Lots of people are in town for the arts festival," the chief said. "Of course, right now most of them are artists. Visitors will start pouring in next week."

"What about Charles Whistler?" Priscilla asked. "Do you suspect him?"

"You bet. He's our number one suspect. When someone runs after a theft..."

"I thought I was your number one suspect," Priscilla said, softly.

"I'm sorry," the chief said, a guilty look on his face. "Generally, I treat everyone as if they're at the top of my list. You wouldn't believe how many confessions I've gotten by doing that. I never really thought you'd taken the painting. You're just not the type. But when we thought we'd found the painting here..."

"Priscilla became your prime suspect?" Joan asked.

"Yeah, I guess so. For about a minute. But then we realized the painting we recovered was a copy. It was dirty. No way someone recently cleaned paint off of it. It sure looked a lot like the original though. Whoever painted it was talented."

"So now Charles has climbed the chart?" Priscilla asked.

"Yes. But to be honest, I'm not convinced he's our man. Mr. Whistler had some problems a few years ago. An addiction to narcotics. He stole to support his habit, but he got help. Turned his life around. I have to wonder if he took off because he was afraid we'd suspect him and the leniency given him in the past would be retracted."

"Til—I mean, no one mentioned that," Joan said.

Priscilla stared aghast at Joan, who had almost said Tilly's name. Joan's face flushed pink at her near mistake. Priscilla glanced at the chief, who seemed somewhat amused by the slip. Although Priscilla was pretty sure he knew exactly who Joan was referring to, he acted as if he hadn't heard her.

"That doesn't mean he didn't do it," the chief said, ignoring Joan's comment. "He found the painting, it disappears, and he leaves town. Pretty suspicious."

"But why didn't he just take it when he realized what it was?" Priscilla said. "Why tell Roxie about it? Let her call you? It doesn't make sense."

"If Roxie had stumbled on his discovery, it might," the chief said. "But according to Roxie that isn't what happened. Charles made a point of letting her know what he'd found. As you say, he could have easily wrapped something around the painting and walked out. No one would have known he had the missing Adair. I have to agree with you that his actions don't point to him as a solid suspect. However, I've seen some pretty dumb things since I entered law enforcement. Maybe taking it didn't occur to him until later. After he'd informed Roxie."

"Maybe," Priscilla said. "But the people we spoke to didn't see him as someone who would do something like this."

"They never do," the chief said with a sigh. "You wouldn't believe how many times I've heard people swearing their family member or friend wasn't capable of a crime. Yet they did it. I think we're all capable of almost anything under the right circumstances."

"That's a rather pessimistic view of people," Joan said.

He nodded. "You're right. After a few years of doing this you find yourself becoming more suspicious of...everyone."

"I'm sorry about that," Priscilla said.

"Well, on the other hand, I've bumped into some very heroic people who were willing to put their lives on the line for others." He shrugged. "Somehow those folks give me the will to keep going."

"I'm glad to hear that," Joan said. "We're blessed to have you as our chief of police."

The chief cleared his throat. "Thank you. And again, I'm sorry about..."

"Nothing to be sorry about," Priscilla said. "I know you were just doing your job." She was happy to feel the tension between her and Chief Westin dissipate. "I have to ask you about Roxie. You've never mentioned her as a suspect."

"Cleared her right away. She has a solid alibi during the time the painting was stolen. She was in her shop, meeting with prospective artists for the festival. Didn't leave the store until late that night."

"Could she have had an accomplice?" Priscilla asked.

"We checked that out, but so far, we haven't found anything to make us think she was working with someone else."

"I'm relieved," Priscilla said. "I like her. So what will you do now?"

He sighed. "We'll keep looking for Charles. I'm going to do some checking on Billy Manders. I need to know more about him. His friends, family. Who could have acquired that painting? We'll have to question people who knew him. Maybe your information will finally lead us in the right direction."

"I think we're all ready to see this end," Priscilla said.

"One thing you didn't tell me," the chief said, frowning. "Do you know who painted over the Adair?"

That part of the story was the other thing Priscilla had left out. Right now, everyone assumed Billy or her mother had done it, but since no one could prove it, Priscilla didn't want to see her mother's reputation sullied.

"No one is certain who did it. Some think it was Billy himself that did it. They have other suspicions, but I really don't want to mention them. We might cast aspersions on an innocent person, and frankly, there's been too much of that lately."

"You're right," the chief said. "If it was someone other than Billy, if they're still living, they'd have to be in their seventies or eighties. I don't want to see someone that old become a target for the FBI. Besides, the statute of limitations ran out a long time ago. They couldn't be prosecuted now anyway."

Priscilla breathed an inward sigh of relief. "I didn't realize that. Thank you, Chief."

Chief Westin stood. "I'd better get going. Just remember that we're keeping an eye on you, Mrs. Grant. If you feel unsafe at any time, just call us. I intend to have a car either watching your house or at least nearby at all times. Until we find out who stole the painting, that is."

"Thank you, Chief. I truly appreciate it."

Joan got up and saw the chief to the front door. When she came back, Priscilla pointed at her. "You really should go home, Joan. I feel perfectly safe now."

Joan frowned at her. "I'm not sure…"

"I'm being protected by the police. Seriously, I'm in good hands." She yawned. "I'm tired and going straight to bed. If I promise to call the police if I hear anything suspicious, will you go home?"

Joan held her hands up in the air. "Okay, I give. I'll go home, but I intend to call you first thing in the morning, before I go to work."

"Fine. I'll keep the phone by my bed. You call me whenever you want to."

Joan came over and put her arms around Priscilla. "You win. But if you change your mind or get nervous being alone, you'll call me, right?"

"Yes, ma'am, I will. You have my word." Priscilla was so beat that she was pretty sure once her head hit the pillow she wouldn't wake up until morning. She truly wasn't worried. If anyone tried to get in, Jake would bark and wake her up.

Priscilla walked Joan and Sister to the door. Then she watched her get into her car and drive away. As Priscilla closed and locked her front door, she couldn't help but reflect on the revelations Tilly, Mildred, and Alma had shared with her. She should probably be upset with her mother, if she truly was the one who painted over the Adair, but it was hard to be angry with her. Her commitment to her friend and her willingness to put herself in possible danger to protect him, made Priscilla feel there was more to the story than the women knew. It was funny. At that moment she felt closer to her mother than she ever had.

CHAPTER TWENTY-FIVE

When Priscilla opened her eyes the next morning, she felt refreshed. She stretched and then swung her legs over the side of the bed. Jake was curled up at the bottom of the bed, one eye open, watching her.

"Good morning," she said. "Thanks for keeping an eye on things." Then she looked up. "And thank You, Father, for keeping me safe. We could sure use Your help finding out who took the painting. Anything You can do would sure be appreciated."

At that moment, Jake let loose with a loud yawn that sounded like someone screeching. It made Priscilla laugh. Jake just looked embarrassed.

"You're something else," she said. "Let's get up and get this day going, okay?"

As if agreeing to her proposition, Jake jumped down from the bed and ran toward the kitchen. After they both had breakfast, Priscilla took him outside for a walk. The air was cool, but not as cold as it had been. Although the forecast was for several more days of rain, a break in the clouds provided a much needed respite. Jake took a little longer than normal, and Priscilla didn't rush him.

On the way back to the house, she noticed a police car drive part way up the road and stop. After she got inside, she looked out the window. The car was still there. The chief was living up to his promise. Oddly, while she felt safer seeing the car out there, knowing she needed protection reminded her that someone had tried to cause her harm. It was a strange feeling. One she certainly didn't enjoy.

Priscilla took a shower and got dressed. Then she dug through a drawer in the kitchen that held phone books for Tisbury and neighboring towns. She found the book for Vineyard Haven. It only took a few seconds to find a number and an address for Cicely Howard. Priscilla wrote the address and the number down and put the note in her purse. She wanted to talk to Dora Genner—and she intended to go alone. Priscilla wasn't certain what she'd hear from Dora and had reservations about sharing what she found out with her cousins. If Dora confirmed that her mother had knowingly painted over a stolen masterpiece... Well, she didn't know if that knowledge was something she wanted to reveal to anyone else. She found herself in a strange dilemma. Priscilla believed in seeking the truth, but she also felt very protective of her mother.

After getting Jake squared away, Priscilla peered out the window again. The police car was gone. Good. The last thing she wanted was to have to explain to the chief where she was going— and why.

She said goodbye to Jake and hurried out to the car. She noticed Tucker's car down by the lighthouse. The weather certainly wasn't cooperating with him. Although it wasn't raining now, it would probably start up soon. She saw him standing near the front of his car, a sketch pad in his hands. He waved at her, and she waved back. Then she got into her car and headed toward

Vineyard Haven. As she drove, she ran her conversation with Tilly, Mildred, and Alma through her mind. It was hard to see them as young women brought together by a love of art. Mildred and Alma certainly had a difficult time getting along now, but when they'd talked about the past, it was as if they remembered, however briefly, that at one time they'd been friends. Maybe coming together to talk to her would help them now. She hoped it was true, but Alma could be rather spiteful, and Mildred was pretty stuck in her ways.

After reaching Vineyard Haven, Priscilla took a couple of wrong turns. Finally, she found the street where Cicely lived. She drove slowly down the street, trying to read house numbers in the rain, which had started up again as predicted. Not the easiest thing to do. She finally found 1430 and pulled into the driveway. She hadn't called because she didn't want to give Dora a chance to refuse to meet with her. Priscilla said a quick prayer, grabbed her umbrella, and got out of the car. She jogged up to the front porch of the small brick ranch home. After ringing the doorbell, she heard someone call out. A few seconds later, the inside door opened. A woman who looked to be in her forties stood in front of the glass storm door, staring at Priscilla, with a quizzical look on her face. She reached out and pulled the storm door open a crack.

"Can I help you?" she asked.

"Are you Cicely Howard?"

The woman nodded.

"My name is Priscilla Grant. My mother, Charlotte Ingerson, was a friend of your mother's. I heard Dora had recently moved here to live with you. I wonder if I could speak to her. I won't stay long."

Although Cicely hesitated a moment, she opened the door the rest of the way. "Please, come in."

Priscilla stepped into a neat living room decorated with home-made touches. Handmade pillows adorned the couch and two overstuffed chairs. A fire burned in the small gas fireplace, and family pictures were lined up on the mantle. It was a charming, cozy room.

"You want to talk to my mother because she and your mother were friends?" Cicely asked.

She had kind eyes. Her nose was sprinkled with freckles, and her brown curly hair was pulled back in a messy bun that framed her heart-shaped face. Priscilla liked her immediately.

"Yes...well, kind of. You see, something happened." Priscilla cleared her throat. She wasn't being clear. "Years ago, your mother and my mother were part of a group of artists."

Cicely's eyes widened. "You mean the Tisbury Collective?"

Surprised, Priscilla nodded. "Yes. You know about it?"

"Oh my, yes. Mom talks about it all the time. She loved being part of that group." Cicely held her hand out. "Can I take your coat?"

"Thank you so much." Priscilla pulled off her wet coat and handed it to Cicely, who hung it up on a long wooden coatrack near the front door.

"Please, sit down. Would you like a cup of coffee? I just made a fresh pot."

Priscilla smiled at her. "I would love it, thanks."

She sat down in one of the chairs while Cicely went into the kitchen to get her coffee. When she came back she had two cups in her hands. "Did you want anything in it?" she asked.

"Black is fine," Priscilla said. "Thank you."

Cicely handed her one of the cups, and Priscilla took it gratefully. She took a sip. "This is delicious," she said. "May I ask what kind of coffee it is?"

"It's a French roast. I grind the beans myself."

"I love different types of coffees, but I'm afraid I'm too lazy to grind beans. The rich taste is certainly worth the effort though."

"I'm glad you like it," Cicely said. "You said something happened? Something that has to do with the collective?"

Priscilla put her cup on the table in front of her. "Yes. A painting has been discovered. A very valuable painting. It was hidden under another painting. We'd hoped someone in the collective would know something about it, but so far we've come up empty. To be honest, your mother is my last hope."

Cicely shook her head. "I doubt she can help you, but I'm sure she'd be happy to talk to you. You said your mother's name was Charlotte?"

"Yes, that's right."

"I distinctly remember Mom mentioning a Charlotte. Let me get her. She's reading in her room."

"Thank you so much. I won't take much of her time."

"Time is something she has too much of," Cicely said. "I'm certain talking to you will be a treat for her. I'll be right back."

Priscilla wasn't sure Dora would see Priscilla's questions as a "treat," but she intended to approach her with gentle caution. The last thing she wanted to do was to offend Dora or cause her distress in any way. As she waited, Priscilla couldn't help but feel a tad nervous. If she couldn't learn anything concrete from Dora, she would probably have to walk away, never knowing the whole story. She would never be certain who stole the painting the first time— or the second time.

A few minutes after she'd left, Cicely came back into the living room accompanied by an older woman. Dora was tall and stately, with silver hair styled in a French twist. Although she walked with a cane, she didn't seem frail. The word that popped into Priscilla's mind was *classy*.

Priscilla stood up. "It's so nice to meet you, Mrs. Genner. My mother was a friend of yours. Charlotte Ingerson?"

Dora's stiff expression softened. "Charlotte. Yes, she was a good friend. I heard she passed away. I'm so sorry."

"Thank you."

Cicely led her mother over to the couch where she sat down. Cicely took a seat next to her. Priscilla really wanted to talk to Dora alone, but it was obvious that wasn't going to happen. She certainly didn't blame Cicely for staying. She would have done the same thing if the situation was reversed. Cicely didn't know Priscilla and was simply looking out for her mother.

"My daughter tells me you have questions about...a painting? We did quite a few paintings during the years the collective existed. I'm not sure I can recall all of them."

Priscilla cleared her throat and considered her next words. How could she bring up the Adair painting without sounding accusatory? Finally, she said, "Do you remember an assignment Adrian Deering gave you? To copy a famous painting?"

Dora smiled. "Yes, I do. I painted Van Gogh's *Starry Night*. I always loved the colors and the flow of that work. It was harder than I anticipated. I'm afraid I didn't come close to the master's technique."

"Actually, it's quite good," Cicely said, patting her mother's hand. "It's hanging in the hallway."

Priscilla smiled at the elderly woman. "Do you happen to recall some of the other paintings members of the collective chose to imitate?"

At this question, Dora frowned. "Let me see...I believe Alma Whitaker chose *Lighthouse at Two Lights* by Edward Hopper. As I remember, she did an adequate job. Tilly Snyder tried to recreate *American Gothic* by Grant Wood." Dora shook her head. "Unfortunately, it did not turn out the way she'd hoped." She stared down at her clasped hands. "I wish I could remember more of them for you, but it was such a long time ago. Besides, as we age, memories seem to become a little distorted. Sometimes they disappear completely."

"What about *Seascape in Shadows* by Arthur Melton Adair?" Priscilla asked.

The reaction was immediate. Dora's expression tightened and she looked away. "I-I'm sorry. I don't remember anything else that could help you. I'm not feeling well today and need to lie down for a while. If you'll excuse me." She grabbed her cane, stood, and walked as quickly as her unsteady legs would carry her. Once she'd left the room, Cicely looked at Priscilla, confusion evident in her expression.

"I'm so sorry," she said slowly. "Sometimes Mom gets a little bewildered, and from time to time she becomes angry for no reason. Please don't take it personally."

"I won't," Priscilla said. "I certainly didn't mean to upset her."

"You didn't get the answer you were looking for, did you?"

"No, unfortunately I didn't."

"Why don't you give me your phone number?" Cicely said. "I'll speak to Mom. If she decides she wants to talk to you, I'll give you a call."

Priscilla reached into her purse and pulled out a card she used for the lighthouse museum. She wrote her cell number on the back, along with the number at the cottage, and handed it to Cicely. "You can reach me at one of these numbers. If I don't answer, just leave a message. I'll call you back as soon as I can." Priscilla stood up. She felt deflated and didn't have much hope that she'd ever hear from Dora.

As Cicely walked her to the door, Priscilla was certain a thief was going to get away with the robbery of a lifetime. And she would never know the role her mother had played in his success.

CHAPTER TWENTY-SIX

As she drove home, Priscilla began to almost hope Charles had taken the painting. Then it wouldn't matter if Dora wouldn't talk to her. She certainly wished the police would find him so they could either recover the painting or rule him out. Perhaps he could answer all the questions that still haunted Priscilla. Of course, there was still the possibility the two thefts weren't connected, but something told her they were. The copy of *Seascape in Shadows* showing up in her kitchen was too much of a coincidence. Her thoughts drifted to Billy, and she wondered if the chief had found any new information about the people in his life. People who might have had access to his painting. Priscilla felt a headache coming on. This entire situation was really confusing. She felt as if all the pieces to this strange mystery were right in front of her but she just couldn't get them to fit together.

As she neared Tisbury, she remembered she had a date with Gerald tonight. Her first reaction was joy, but then she remembered that he might be leaving. Joy quickly dissipated and an almost overwhelming sadness engulfed her. She was certain she wouldn't see him much if he moved. She wanted to accept whatever happened as God's will and move on, but there was something inside her that wanted to fight back. Make him stay. Several times she'd seen something in him. Something that made her think he had feelings for her. Had she just seen what she wanted to? Was she deceiving herself?

She entered Tisbury and took the turn that would lead her home. As she neared the cottage, she saw the chief's car parked outside. What now? She pulled up next to him and got out. He opened his door and walked over to where she waited. The rain had turned into a light drizzle.

"Hi, Chief. Come on in," Priscilla said.

She wanted to be alone, but she couldn't ask the chief to leave. She unlocked her door. Jake was waiting on the other side, happy to see her. He allowed Chief Westin to pet him and then followed Priscilla as she hung up her coat.

"Can I get you something to drink?" she asked.

"No. I won't stay long. I just thought you might like to know that Charles Whistler turned himself in."

Priscilla's mouth dropped open in surprise. "Does he have the painting?"

The chief shook his head. "No. And I don't think he took it. He left for the reasons I suspected. Was afraid he'd be charged with theft because of his past. He was holed up in a motel in Edgartown. Under a different name. The motel owner says he never left his room from the time he checked in. That means he couldn't have tried to run you off the cliff. Or put the fake painting in your house."

"Is he in jail?"

"Yes," the chief said. "We searched his motel room from top to bottom. And his car. No painting. Not even the slightest sign he ever had it. I'm not saying it's impossible. He could have dumped it somewhere—or given it to an accomplice. Maybe his accomplice is the person who's been terrorizing you. We're still checking that out. But I just can't see it. We can't find anyone connected to him who could have done these things. Besides, this man fought hard to clean up his life. He's done everything he could to heal his relationship with his children. He's not rich, but he has some money put away. He has a comfortable life. Why ruin it now?"

"Could I talk to him?" Priscilla asked.

Chief Westin gave her a quick smile. "Why do you think I'm telling you where he is?"

Priscilla laughed lightly. "Thanks. I appreciate it."

"I'm not doing it out of the goodness of my heart. I think you might be able to get him to talk to you. Tell you the truth. If there's any truth still yet to be told."

"Thanks. I could be down there in...say an hour or so?"

"He'll be there, but I can only hold him for twenty-four hours without charging him."

"Okay. Thanks. And thanks for protecting me. I truly appreciate it."

Chief Westin shrugged. "It's the least I can do." He put his hat on and strode over to the door and left without saying anything else.

Priscilla stared at the door for a while. Interesting. Maybe she could learn something from Charles. She needed some hope after her visit with Dora. She looked over at Jake, who stared at her as if he had an opinion about the whole thing. His expression made her laugh.

"Let's take a quick walk," she told him. "Then I'm going to the station. Maybe Charles can shed some light on who took the painting."

They didn't stay outside long. Although the rain was only a light drizzle, Jake wasn't a fan. When they got back, Priscilla dried him off, got him settled, and then drove to the police department in Tisbury. She pulled up to the large white clapboard building that housed the police department and the ambulance service. She got out and went inside. Gabrielle Grimes greeted her with a smile.

"Hello, Priscilla. What can I help you with today?"

Gabrielle was the first person visitors encountered when entering the station. She used her index finger to push her large black glasses back from the tip of her nose.

"Chief Westin said you've got Charles Whistler here. I'd like to talk to him if possible."

Gabrielle nodded. "He told me you might stop by." She picked up the phone on her desk. "April," she said, "Mrs. Grant is here to see Mr. Whistler. Would you escort her back to our holding cell?" Whatever April said seemed to satisfy her. She said thank you and hung up. "Officer Brown will take you to see him."

"Thanks, Gabrielle."

"I hope they find that painting," Gabrielle said. "I can't believe the back door was unlocked." She leaned forward as if wanting to tell Priscilla a secret. Priscilla stepped up closer to the desk. "The janitor leaves it unlocked sometimes. We've told him time and time again to make sure he locks it behind him. But...Well, he's almost seventy. I think he just forgets."

"Sounds like you need to get a new janitor," Priscilla said softly.

Gabrielle's eyes widened, and her eyebrows shot up. "Manny's been with us . . . forever. I don't think the chief would fire him."

Priscilla couldn't hold back a smile. The Tisbury Police Department was excellent. She'd put them up against any police force in the country. But in a town like Tisbury, people mattered more than procedure. She suspected Manny would be with them until he died—or decided to retire. Whichever came first.

"I understand," she said to Gabrielle.

The door behind Gabrielle swung open and Officer April Brown entered the lobby. "Hello, Mrs. Grant. I'll take you back to see Mr. Whistler."

"Thank you." Priscilla said goodbye to Gabrielle and followed April through the door and down a long hallway filled with rooms. Some were offices. Others were used for meetings or to question suspects. Her heart beat a little faster than normal when they passed the room where she had been kept when she was under arrest yesterday. They turned a corner and walked past a large storage area. A few steps later they came upon the cells. Charles sat in one of them. He looked up as they approached.

"I can't let you in with him," April said. "You'll have to talk to him through the bars." She retrieved a chair that sat against the wall. She pulled it up near the cell. "You can sit here."

"Thank you, April," Priscilla said. April was a no-nonsense officer, yet she tried to be kind. Her husband and her two teenage sons adored her.

April nodded. "I'll be back in…" She looked down at her watch. "Twenty minutes? Is that enough time?"

"More than enough. I appreciate it."

"You're welcome." April turned and walked down the hallway, leaving Priscilla alone with Charles.

She sat down in the chair. Charles was perched on the edge of the cot in his cell. He was only a few feet away from her.

"I'm sorry if I caused you any trouble," he said before Priscilla had a chance to say anything. "I shouldn't have taken off like that." He stared down at the floor. "I had some problems a few years ago. I was afraid the police would think I took the painting."

"Can I ask where you were when the painting was stolen?" Priscilla asked.

"I was at home. Alone." He shook his head. "I don't have an alibi."

"You live alone?"

"Yes, ma'am. I have grown children who live in town, but my wife left me because of my…problem. I'm not the same man I was but it will take some time for her to trust me again…if she ever does." He gazed around his cell. "This certainly won't help."

"I'm sorry," Priscilla said. "If it comforts you, I don't think you took the painting and neither does the chief."

The corners of Charles's mouth ticked up. "I know he thinks I'm innocent. He won't say so—because he can't, I guess—but it's pretty obvious he doesn't believe I'm a thief. I can't tell you how much that means to me."

"I suspect you won't be here much longer, Charles." Priscilla paused for a moment and looked around her. Not seeing anyone, she scooted her chair a little closer to the cell bars. "Charles, I need to ask you something. About the Tisbury Collective."

His bushy gray eyebrows shot up, and he stood to his feet. "Mrs. Grant, I'm sorry, but I can't talk about that. I—I need you to leave now. Please."

CHAPTER TWENTY-SEVEN

Priscilla stayed in her chair and frowned at Charles. This was the second time she'd gotten the same reaction in one day. Frankly, she was getting tired of it.

"Look, I'm not planning to get anyone in trouble. I just need to know the truth. My mother was Charlotte Ingerson. And my aunt was Marjorie Latham. Right now, they're implicated in the theft of the Adair painting. Or at least suspected of being involved in a cover up after the theft. I want to clear their names if I can. Or face the truth if that's what it takes. I spoke to Dora Genner this morning. You knew her as Dora Metcalf. Her reaction was exactly like yours. Why? Unless you stole the painting, you shouldn't have anything to worry about. You know the statute of limitations protects you from the original theft. The one that happened fifty years ago?"

Charles turned around, not facing Priscilla. After a pause, he went back to his cot and sat down again. "I hear what you're saying, but you don't know everything. I—I can't take the risk. I'm sorry, Mrs. Grant. I really am."

"Does this have anything to do with Billy Manders?" Priscilla asked.

A shiver moved through Charles's body at the mention of Billy's name, and the color drained from his face.

"He's dead, you know," Priscilla said. "He can't hurt you anymore."

"I know he's dead. You don't understand."

Priscilla scooted her chair a little closer. "Look, Charles. You're a good man. I can tell that. Do you really want the person who took the Adair painting fifty years ago—or two days ago—to get away with it? As someone who so appreciates art, I would think you'd want him—or her—caught and the painting sent back to New York where millions of people can enjoy it."

"Of course I want it recovered. Art should be enjoyed by everyone. But I—I just can't help you."

Priscilla sighed in frustration. "I'm sorry. I just don't understand. There's no one left to be afraid of."

Charles turned his head and fixed his gaze on Priscilla. "And how do you know that, Mrs. Grant? Sometimes when a bad person dies, there's someone else waiting to pick up where he left off."

"Are you telling me that you've been threatened?"

Charles looked away from her. "I'm not telling you anything. I'll thank you to leave me in peace now. I'm sorry."

It was clear there was nothing Priscilla could say to get him to talk to her. She stood up and pushed the chair back against the wall where April had gotten it. "If you change your mind, please contact me," she said. "The chief has my number."

When she got no response, she walked away, turning toward the hallway April had led her down. At the end of the hall she found April leaning against the wall. She noticed Priscilla approaching. "That was quick. I take it things didn't go well?"

"No, he's afraid to tell anyone what he knows. I can't understand it. It's been fifty years since the original theft. The statute of limitations has long passed, but he's still afraid. He implied that there might be someone else. Someone who is threatening him."

"Remember that someone brought the copy of *Seascape in Shadows* to Tisbury," April said. "Maybe this person is intimidating anyone who could shed some light on what really happened."

"I guess that could be true. It would explain Charles's reaction." She frowned at April. "The chief said he was checking out Billy's friends and family. Has he found anything?"

April shrugged. "I haven't heard anything. I'm sure if he discovers something important he'll let you know."

"I hope so." Priscilla glanced at the chief's door, which was closed. "Is he in?"

April nodded. "I think he's working on reports. Let me see if he can talk to you for a few minutes." She emphasized the words *a few minutes,* making it clear that Priscilla shouldn't stay too long.

She waited as April approached Chief Westin's door and knocked. Priscilla heard the chief's gruff voice from the other side. April opened it and went in, closing it behind her. A few seconds later, she came out and gestured to Priscilla. "He says he can talk to you. Not too long, okay? He needs to get through these reports."

The second warning. Priscilla nodded. "I won't take long. I promise."

April smiled, and her face relaxed. She held the door open and ushered Priscilla through. When she entered the chief's office,

Priscilla found him behind his battle-scarred desk, a large stack of folders on one side, a small pile on the other side. Priscilla guessed by the chief's tense expression that the shorter stack was his completed work. It was clear that police work was more than just arresting people and chasing criminals.

"What can I do for you, Mrs. Grant?" the chief asked. His eyebrows were drawn together in a scowl that almost looked permanent. Maybe it was.

"I spoke to Charles," she said, standing near the door, "but he wouldn't tell me anything. He's afraid, Chief. Is it possible he's being threatened by someone? With Billy dead, I'm wondering who that might be. Were you able to find out anything about his family? Or did you uncover any acquaintances who might be trying to pressure Charles?"

The chief riffled through the larger stack of files on his desk until he uncovered the one he wanted. He pulled it out and searched through it until he found a particular piece of paper. He pulled it out of the file and read through it. "I'm sorry, Mrs. Grant. Everything in that direction seems to lead nowhere. But you might be interested to know that we also checked out the other two men who the ladies said went to Plymouth for the exhibit. Raymond Hill was married, but his wife died a few years before he did. There was a son, but he moved away years ago. So far we haven't been able to find him." The chief stared at the page again. "The last place Raymond and his son lived was Boston. I've asked the Boston police to talk to his old neighbors—if they're still there, that is. If I hear anything, I'll let you know."

"And I told you already that Adrian Deering is in a nursing home here on the island."

"Yes. From what you told me, it doesn't seem like we'd get much from him that would be helpful."

Priscilla clasped her hands together and sighed. "One dead end after another."

"It happens, Mrs. Grant. All we can do is the best we can do."

"I know you're right, Chief. I just keep feeling like we're missing something. That the answer is right in front of us."

Chief Westin chuckled. "When most people say that, I probably wouldn't take it too seriously. But when it comes from you... We'll keep trying. I'll let you know if I come up with anything new. You do the same for me, okay?"

Priscilla nodded. She hadn't told the chief about Dora, but since nothing had come from her visit, what did it matter?

After saying goodbye to the chief, Priscilla walked out of the police station. It was still raining. Would it ever stop? She had no idea what to do next. Maybe some people would always suspect her aunt of being involved with the theft of the stolen painting. Although it shouldn't bother her, it did. Marjorie Latham was a wonderful woman whose reputation shouldn't be damaged by something she had nothing to do with. Priscilla was certain Marjorie hadn't known anything about the painting. But when it came to her own mother, she wasn't sure what to think.

Priscilla got into her car and was just getting ready to start the engine when her phone rang. She fished it out of her purse and answered the call.

"Mrs. Grant?" a voice said. "This is Cicely Howard. I'm so sorry to bother you, but my mother is very upset. She wants to know if you'll come back. She says she needs to talk to you."

After telling Cicely she would be happy to return, Priscilla disconnected the call. She sat there for a few minutes, watching the rain come down. Could this be it? Did Dora have the answers they'd been looking for?

She started her car and headed back to Vineyard Haven.

CHAPTER TWENTY-EIGHT

On the way to Cicely's house, Priscilla tried to imagine what Dora would tell her. She also worried that Dora was being threatened like Charles. Could she be putting herself in danger? It was almost two o'clock when Priscilla got to Vineyard Haven. She hadn't eaten lunch and her stomach was growling, so she pulled into a fast food restaurant. A hastily consumed double cheeseburger, fries, and a soft drink fortified her. Not the healthiest meal, but at least her stomach wouldn't make embarrassing noises when she talked to Dora.

When she pulled into Cicely's driveway, she noticed Dora standing at the large picture window at the front of the house. She quickly let go of the drapes when she realized Priscilla saw her.

Priscilla got out of the car, ran to the covered front porch, and rang the doorbell. Cicely opened the door immediately.

"Thank you so much for coming back," she said. "Mom is determined to talk to you. She says she must tell you the truth, whatever that means."

"All right," Priscilla said as she stepped into Cicely's living room. Dora sat in a chair next to the couch.

"Let me get you something to drink," Cicely said, "and then I guess I'll find something else to do. Mom wants to talk to you ... alone."

Priscilla nodded. "I don't need anything to drink, thanks."

"Okay." Cicely looked at her mother. "Mom? Do you want anything?"

"If you'd bring my coffee from the kitchen, that would be wonderful. Thank you, honey."

Priscilla and Dora sat quietly in the living room while Cicely went to the kitchen. A few seconds later, she came back with Dora's coffee cup, which she set on the table in front of her mother.

"Thanks, dear," Dora said. "I'll let you know when we're done."

It was obvious Cicely was curious about what her mother wanted to tell Priscilla, but she didn't argue. Instead she turned around and left the room.

"I'm sorry to make you come back a second time," Dora said. "When you showed up this morning, I simply reacted. I didn't have time to think. Once you left, I realized there was no reason to hide the truth any longer."

Priscilla felt her muscles tighten. Did Dora really know what happened all those years ago?

As if she could tell what Priscilla was thinking, Dora sighed. "Some of what I tell you might disturb you, but if I can explain it correctly, I hope you'll understand why we did what we did."

"I'm listening," Priscilla said.

"Before I tell you about what happened back then, I have to ask why it matters now?"

"I'd asked you about the paintings the members of the collective did for Adrian Deering?" Priscilla said. "The copies?"

Dora nodded. She seemed anxious, as if talking to Priscilla was hard for her.

"My aunt, Marjorie Latham, had a painting that hung over her fireplace—now my fireplace since she left her property to me when she passed away. The painting was of the cottage and the lighthouse that has been in our family for many years. I took the painting in to be cleaned. The person cleaning the painting, Charles Whistler, I believe you know him, found another painting under it. The original *Seascape in Shadows* by Arthur Melton Adair. The painting was stolen fifty years ago from a traveling exhibit in Plymouth. Once it was discovered, my aunt and I were both under suspicion of being involved with the theft. As you can imagine, this has been most disconcerting. I'm simply trying to find the truth. Discover how the painting ended up where it did, and find the person who originally stole the Adair."

"What do you mean by *originally*?" Dora asked.

"Once the painting was recovered, it was stolen again. Then someone planted the copy—the one done by Billy Manders—in my home. They were trying to make it look as if I'd stolen the painting."

"But that doesn't make sense," Dora said, frowning. "It wouldn't take experts long to see that the copy wasn't the original."

"I agree. And it didn't. But now we have to ask ourselves how someone managed to acquire the copy. Supposedly Billy took it with him when he left town. I'm beginning to wonder if that's true. Maybe someone else had it. Someone still alive."

"Billy is dead?" Dora asked, her eyebrows arching in surprise. "I didn't know that."

"Yes, he is. He died almost ten years ago. I take it you didn't keep in touch with other members of the collective?"

She shook her head. "No. I tried to put that time of my life behind me."

"Do you mind if I ask why?"

Dora's small smile was sad. "We were all close friends at one time. But then we decided..." She took a deep, shaky breath and shook her head. "I can't believe I'm talking about this, but it's time the truth came out. First of all, do you mind if I ask how you learned about the collective and the assignment we had from Adrian?"

"Originally, I spoke to Mildred Pearson. She told me about the Tisbury Collective. Since then, I've also talked to Tilly Snyder, Alma Whitaker, and Charles Whistler. Tilly, Mildred, and Alma were the most forthcoming about Billy, but they didn't know everything."

"I see," Dora said.

Priscilla sat still, almost afraid to move. She wanted to hear what Dora had to say—yet she was also a little afraid to learn the truth.

"You mentioned the assignment given to us by Adrian Deering. Yes, Billy Manders chose *Seascape in Shadows* as the painting he wanted to copy. After the assignment, we learned that the Metropolitan Museum of Art had a touring exhibit of paintings that would spend some time in Plymouth. One of the paintings was *Seascape in Shadows*. Probably chosen because it was painted not far from here. Adair was primarily a New England painter, you know." She stopped for a moment to pick up her coffee cup. She took a drink and set it down. It was as if she were hoping coffee would give her courage. But of course, it couldn't do that.

"Most of us wanted to go to the exhibit, but we were working. Or we had other responsibilities. Your mother had you to take care of, and she didn't feel it was right to leave for several days when she was in town to visit family. Only three people ended up going. Raymond, Billy, and Adrian. They were gone for three days. When they came back, we could all tell something was wrong. Raymond was quiet. Too quiet. And Billy seemed upset. It was clear he didn't want to be near Raymond. I couldn't tell much from Adrian. He was just...Adrian." She cleared her throat and stared at her coffee cup again. Then she said, "Not long after they returned, the story hit the papers, that *Seascape in Shadows* had been stolen. It was in storage and hadn't been hung up yet. Raymond, Billy, and Adrian told us they hadn't seen it. That Billy's friend wasn't able to get them into the part of the museum where the painting was being kept. Although it was awful—that someone had taken the Adair—none of us thought much about it. Until Tilly Snyder mentioned that she'd tried to buy Billy's copy of *Seascape in Shadows* before they went to Plymouth. He wanted to sell it, but Raymond told Tilly it wasn't for sale. He was very rude about it. Tilly's family had money, and she'd offered a rather large amount. We all knew Billy needed the money, but he gave in to Raymond and told Tilly he couldn't let her have it. Then I found out that Raymond took the painting with him when they went to Plymouth. That really raised my suspicions."

Priscilla's thoughts were reeling. Surely Dora was a bit confused. "Wait...you mean Billy, right? *Billy* took the painting with him when they went to Plymouth."

Dora shook her head. "No, I mean Raymond. You see, Raymond had a gambling problem. We'd all loaned him money from time to time. He never paid us back, of course. Let's just say that Raymond's actions seemed dubious at best." Once again she picked up her cup and took a slow sip. This time she held it in her hands rather than setting it back down. "Raymond left town not long after he, Billy, and Adrian came back from Plymouth. A few months later, your mother and Marjorie had a huge falling-out. I understand that they never made up." Dora blinked several times, and her voice broke. "I hate that they threw away their relationship for nothing."

"What do you mean, for nothing?" Priscilla asked.

"Billy and your mother were very close friends. I stress the word *friends*. There was never anything romantic between them, but your aunt misunderstood. After Billy came back from Plymouth, it was obvious he was very distressed. Whatever it was, he wouldn't talk to anyone about it. Except your mother."

"You think he told her what had happened?"

"I know he did," Dora said.

Priscilla frowned at her. "How would you know that for certain?"

Dora raised her face, and her eyes met Priscilla's. "Because the last time she was in town, after her argument with Marjorie, your mother told me everything."

CHAPTER TWENTY-NINE

Priscilla couldn't tear her gaze away from Dora. She was finally going to hear the whole story. Excitement mixed with dread. Would what she heard change the way she saw her mother—and Aunt Marjorie? Even so, she had to know the truth.

"Will you tell it to me?" she asked Dora.

Dora nodded. "I'll tell you what your mother told me if you want to hear it. I'm not betraying her trust now that she's gone."

"I would like to hear it. Please."

"All right." Dora sighed again and put down the cup she'd been clutching. She clasped her hands together. "As I said, your mother and I were good friends. Not as close as she was with Billy, but still . . . close. Your mother trusted me, and she didn't trust a lot of people."

Dora was telling the truth. Priscilla's mother hadn't let a lot of people into her life. When she had, they were people she believed were true friends. She'd always been a bit suspicious of people overall.

"After Raymond left town, the group broke up. Everyone knew something was wrong. We had our suspicions, but to be honest, I don't think any of us really wanted to know the truth. If we did, we'd be responsible for it. And now it seems we had

differing ideas about who the guilty party was. I think it's the reason the collective disbanded. Fear and self-protection. Adrian was
saddened to see people leave. To this day, I can't tell you if he knew
what happened in Plymouth. I honestly have no idea."

"What happened to the Adair?" Priscilla asked. The question
slipped out before she realized it. She didn't want to push Dora too
far. She was afraid she might change her mind. But Dora didn't
seem surprised by Priscilla's query.

"Before she left town for the last time, your mother came to
me. She told me she'd painted something for your aunt. She asked
me to deliver it along with a letter that said it was from a secret
admirer. She didn't want to take a chance that Marjorie would see
her. If Marjorie caught me, I was supposed to tell her that Billy
gave it to me. That he painted it for her before he left town." Dora
shivered, but the room was very warm. Too warm, in fact. "She
never told me the Adair was under it. I was suspicious, but she
didn't offer the information and I didn't ask. I didn't want to
know. As I'm sure you can understand, I was afraid that knowing
too much might make me complicit in the theft. Your mother
would never put me in that kind of position." She took a deep
breath before continuing. "Billy told your mother that Raymond
insisted on taking his copy of *Seascape in Shadows* to Plymouth.
He wouldn't allow Billy to sell it. Basically, he stole it from Billy.
When they returned, Billy confronted Raymond, who told him
what occurred in Plymouth. It seems Raymond also had a contact
at the museum, one that was only too willing to help him steal the
Adair. The idea was to switch the copy for the real painting.

Raymond knew the museum would figure out they had a fake, but not right away. He had a buyer lined up to purchase the Adair painting. Some guy who worked with rich people who like to acquire famous artwork for their own enjoyment. But something went wrong. I don't know exactly what happened. Billy didn't either. Raymond and his friend got the Adair, but couldn't get the copy in before the theft was noticed. So Raymond left Plymouth with both paintings."

"What about the guy who worked for the museum?"

"Billy said Raymond threatened him. Told him he'd tell the authorities he was the one who set everything up. The man didn't want to lose his job—or go to prison for theft. So he kept quiet. Never told anyone as far as I know."

"So Raymond brought both paintings back to Tisbury?"

Dora nodded. "He still planned to sell the Adair to his contact. Let me say that Billy didn't know any of this until they got back from their trip. He had no idea that Raymond had the original Adair. When Raymond told him, Billy made it clear that if he didn't return the painting and turn himself in, he would contact the police himself. That's when everything changed."

"What do you mean?"

"According to Charlotte, Raymond told Billy he'd blame the whole thing on him. He would tell the authorities that Billy was the one who'd taken the painting." Dora shrugged. "There was no way for Billy to prove he was innocent. The only other person who knew Raymond took the painting wasn't talking. Billy was frightened. He was convinced no one would believe the truth. After all, he'd painted the copy. It made him look guilty. Billy didn't want to go to prison."

"Raymond would have gone too."

"Yes, but that wouldn't have changed anything for Billy. He wasn't a weak man, but he was nice. You know, kind. Mild. Not the kind of person to do well in prison."

Priscilla nodded. "So then what happened?"

"That's all I know, Priscilla. Except that someone took the Adair painting from Raymond. I can't tell you who it was because I really don't know. Then your mother asked me to give Marjorie the painting she did of the lighthouse and the cottage." She shrugged. "You'll have to draw your own conclusions."

"You believe she took the Adair and painted over it."

"I don't know. Maybe Billy really did paint over it. There's no way for any of us to know for certain. Regardless, I believe your mother knew the Adair was under the painting she gave your aunt. I'm sure she was tortured over that knowledge. She believed the painting should go back to the museum in New York, but she was more afraid for her friend. Again, I can't prove this. Your mother was careful to protect me. To protect everyone. I did what she asked and dropped the painting off at the cottage with a note that said it was from a secret admirer. I believe your mother originally planned to come back one day. Retrieve the painting and make things right. But then she and your aunt had that final argument at Thanksgiving. Charlotte never came back to the island after that." Dora frowned. "I'm sure it never occurred to her that you would someday inherit the Latham property. If it had, she probably wouldn't have left the painting with your aunt. The last thing she'd want to do would be to drag you into this."

"My aunt regretted her fight with my mother. I think leaving the property to me was a way to bridge the gap between them."

"Charlotte had no way of knowing that her decision would put you in the bull's eye when the Adair was discovered."

Priscilla shook her head. "No, she didn't. Did you ever talk to her about the painting? After she left that summer, I mean?"

"Only once. We phoned each other occasionally. Tried to stay in touch, but she never brought up the painting. Or Billy. But she called me..." Dora hesitated a moment. Priscilla could see the conflict on her face.

"Tell me."

"Charlotte called me about a week before she died. She still didn't admit that she'd taken the painting. But she did tell me she felt guilty about a decision she'd made. Before she hung up she said, 'Dora, I won't be around much longer. I want you to know that if there's anything you want to do—anything you want to say—you have my blessing. I'm leaving it up to you.' Although she never told me the Adair was under the other painting, I knew she was telling me I could call the authorities and tell them what she'd done. At that time, Billy was still alive. So was Raymond. In the end, I left it alone. You see, not only would it have affected Billy, but I was afraid the rest of us could be implicated as well. I just couldn't do it. The truth has haunted me all these years. I wanted it to come out. And now it has." Dora leaned closer to Priscilla and then reached out and took her hand. "Your mother died keeping her terrible secret. You have to know that what she did, she did out of love. You might think what she did was dishonest, but she didn't benefit from the theft of the Adair. The truth is, she suffered because of it."

"Raymond never suspected what my mother did?" she asked.

Dora withdrew her hand and leaned back. "No, and no one told him about the painting given to your aunt. Would he have realized it was the Adair? I have no idea. All Raymond knew was that he got up one morning to find his precious painting gone. Charlotte suspected that one of the reasons Raymond left town was because the man who was supposed to buy the painting was very powerful—and violent. It's possible he would have retaliated against Raymond if he didn't get his painting."

"After Raymond left, did any of you ever hear from him again?"

Dora shook her head. "No. I have no idea where he is, and I haven't heard from anyone else in the collective in all these years. Except your mother, of course."

"Actually, Raymond passed away a few months ago."

Dora didn't look surprised, she just nodded. "I never wanted to see him again. I guess I don't have to worry about that anymore."

"Dora, you know that *Seascape in Shadows* was stolen from the police department, don't you?"

"Oh, yes. It's the talk of Tisbury."

"Do you have any idea who might have taken it?"

Dora shrugged. "I have absolutely no idea, Priscilla. I certainly wouldn't suspect anyone from the collective. The entire town knew about the painting. It could be anyone. I'm shocked someone was able to break into the police station and steal it. That painting should have been properly secured."

"I agree," Priscilla said. "We have a great police department. Someone made a mistake, and, unfortunately it happened at the worst possible time. It seems the maintenance man forgot to lock the back door. This wasn't the first time it had happened." Priscilla stood up. "I've taken enough of your time," she said. "I can't thank you enough for being candid with me. I may not know who has the Adair, but at least I finally know what happened all those years ago."

"What will you do with the knowledge?"

Priscilla had been wondering the same thing. Did she have a responsibility to tell Chief Westin what she'd learned? Raymond was dead. So was Billy. No one could be prosecuted now. Would the truth embarrass people who were her friends? "I honestly don't know," she said finally. "But when I make a decision, I'll let you know."

"You do whatever you feel you need to." Dora smiled sadly. "My daughter took me in because I'm ill. I don't know how much more time I have. At this point, I'm not afraid of what any man can do to me. I just want to make sure I'm right with God."

"I'm sorry," Priscilla said. "Please, if I can do anything…"

"There is one thing I'd like," Dora said. "I'd love to see my old friends again. Those who want to see me anyway. I think Tilly might be happy to see me. Not sure about anyone else."

"I'll do what I can," Priscilla said. "You have my word."

"Thank you." Dora started to get up, but Priscilla stopped her. "I can show myself out. Thank you again, Dora."

"You're welcome."

Priscilla walked to the front door and opened it. When she shut it behind her, she stood on the porch and watched the rain come down. It would take some time for her to take in everything Dora had told her. The relief she felt in knowing that her mother had acted to protect an innocent man instead of a guilty one was overwhelming. She had a lot to take into consideration before she could decide what to do next.

CHAPTER THIRTY

When Priscilla got home she noticed Tucker's car parked near the lighthouse, but she didn't see him anywhere. Maybe he was inside the car. The rain had finally stopped and although the skies were cloudy, at least it wasn't terribly cold. This seemed like a good time to finish his sketch. She thought about driving over to see how he was doing. Usually she loved seeing sketches and paintings of her lighthouse. But right now she was afraid it would only remind her of her mother's painting. Instead she decided to go inside and call Joan. She wanted to tell her what Dora had said and see what she thought. It was almost four o'clock. Tonight she was having dinner with Gerald, and she needed time to get ready. Although she was excited to see him, she was also a little afraid. Afraid he would confirm that he was moving away. How should she react? Could she smile and tell him she thought he was doing the right thing when her heart was breaking?

When she got inside, she took off her coat, got a cup of coffee, and dialed Joan's number. When she answered, Priscilla started telling her about Dora, but before she got very far, Joan interrupted her.

"You didn't tell me you were going to talk to her. I would have come with you."

"I wasn't sure what she was going to say," Priscilla said. "I wanted to hear it first. In case she shared something upsetting."

"Like saying Aunt Marjorie stole the Adair?"

"Yeah, exactly like that."

There was a long pause. Then Joan said, "Did she steal it?"

"No, Joan," Priscilla said. "Aunt Marjorie wasn't a master criminal. Raymond Hill was the thief. She confirmed a lot of what Tilly, Alma, and Mildred suspected but about Raymond, not Billy. Mom and Billy were both afraid that he would be blamed for the theft."

"That's amazing!" Joan exclaimed. "I wonder how Tilly, Mildred, and Alma will take the news that they've blamed the wrong man all these years? Do you think this could be what your aunt and your mom argued about?"

"I think the reason Mom and Aunt Marjorie argued that summer before their final blowout was because Aunt Marjorie was convinced Mom and Billy were having an affair."

Joan sighed. "Marjorie should have known better. Your mother loved your father. Besides, she wasn't that kind of person."

Priscilla smiled at Joan's comment. "Thank you for saying that. I agree." She sighed. "I assume Aunt Marjorie still believed Mom had stolen Billy from her when they were younger. It seems jealousy reared its ugly head and contributed to Marjorie's suspicions. The truth was, Mom was trying to help Billy. They really were close friends. They spent a lot of time together that summer. That's why Marjorie jumped to the conclusion that something untoward was going on."

"Untoward, huh?"

"Oh, hush. Would you rather I said something *fishy*?"

"At least it wouldn't sound like it came out of the mouth of someone over ninety."

Priscilla made a sound designed to let her cousin know she didn't appreciate being called old. "Anyway..." she said. "I never could figure out why Mom and Marjorie would fight over someone when Mom was happily married. Now I know for certain why it happened."

"I guess it makes sense, but it certainly is sad that they couldn't have worked things out before they died."

"I know. I feel the same way. At least we know the truth now."

"You're right," Joan said. "What else did Dora say?"

Priscilla gave her the short version. "There's more," she said when she'd finished, "but I don't have time to talk about it now. We need to get together. You, me, Trudy, and Gail."

"What about tonight?"

"I can't. I've got a date with Gerald."

"How about lunch tomorrow?" Joan asked.

"Okay. Why don't we go back to the Inn? I need to talk to Tilly."

"I guess so. We're there so much we might as well buy our own table," Joan said. "I'll call everyone. Hopefully Gail can get away."

"Okay. See you tomorrow."

After she disconnected the call, Priscilla sat and stared at her phone for a while. It had certainly been a busy day. She wondered if she could call off her date with Gerald tonight. But no matter how she tried to frame an excuse, her reasons sounded lame. Maybe it would be best to see him and put an end to things. Not that they'd admitted there was a *thing*. Priscilla needed him to tell her he was leaving and that they wouldn't see each other anymore. She needed to move on—although she wasn't sure what that meant. She wasn't looking for a boyfriend when she met Gerald. Feelings for him sort of snuck up on her. Facing the knowledge that he was going away made it clear that she was more attached to him than she'd realized. Losing him would hurt. A lot. A tear snuck out of the corner of her eye. She quickly wiped it away.

"No time for that, Priscilla," she said out loud. Jake turned his head sideways as if trying to understand what she was saying. "I'm okay, Jake," she said softly.

After taking Jake out, Priscilla decided to take a hot shower to relax. She felt tense. After getting into the shower, she let the water wash over her until she felt better. When she got out she wrapped a towel around herself and went to the closet. What should she wear? She looked at a couple of dresses but they didn't feel like the right choice. Finally, she chose a dark blue wool skirt and a cream-colored sweater with tiny gold threads running through it, giving it a shimmering effect. Although she usually wore flats, she had a pair of dark blue pumps that went well with the skirt. After getting dressed, she looked in the mirror. Her chin-length light brown hair looked so plain. She rummaged around in the bottom drawer of her dressing table until she found a rarely used curling iron. She plugged it in, not certain if it still worked, but sure enough, it started to get hot. She used it to put some curl in her hair. When she was done, she liked the way her hair looked. Since it had been raining a lot, she used a little hair spray, hoping it would keep her curls from going flat. Then she pulled out her makeup bag. A little light blue eye shadow, some dark blue eyeliner, and some mascara. A tube of shimmery pink lipstick completed her efforts. When she finished, she cast a critical eye on the results. She had to admit that she looked pretty good. "Not bad for someone pushing sixty," she said to her image.

She got up from her dressing table wondering why she cared so much about how she looked tonight. Was she hoping Gerald would decide not to leave? For a moment, she considered removing her makeup and changing into something plainer. But a voice inside told her not to do it. It wasn't wrong to want to look nice, Gerald or no Gerald.

She was just putting her curling iron away when all the lights suddenly went out. The sun had set so the house was totally dark. Jake began to bark.

"It's okay," Priscilla said, trying to calm him. She felt her way from the bedroom into the kitchen where she had flashlights and battery-operated lanterns for situations just like this. Losing power out here wasn't unusual, and she was prepared.

But as she reached into her cabinet to get a flashlight, she heard a noise. Priscilla straightened up and stared at her side door. Someone was rattling the doorknob, trying to get in. Jake raced over to the door and began to bark furiously. The rattling stopped, but Priscilla was too frightened to move. Who was trying to get in, and where were they now? Could they have gone to the front door?

She finally turned and walked slowly toward the front of the cottage, the long metal flashlight clutched in her hand like a weapon. As she advanced toward the door, Jake ran in front of her. He sniffed at the bottom of the door, but he didn't bark. Did that mean no one was there? Priscilla stood there for a while, waiting for someone to try the front door, but nothing happened. She felt her way to the coffee table where she'd left her cell phone. The landline wouldn't work without electricity, but her cell phone should. She started to dial 911, when suddenly someone pounded loudly on the door. Priscilla screamed as her cell phone slipped out of her hand and hit the floor. It lay in pieces at her feet.

CHAPTER THIRTY-ONE

Crying, she bent down, trying to put her shattered phone back together. Now she had no way to call for help. As she knelt there, trying to figure out what to do, the person standing at the front door called out.

"Mrs. Grant? It's Chief Westin. Are you okay?"

Almost weak with relief, Priscilla got up and raced to the door, flinging it open. The chief stood there, highlighted by the headlights of his car.

"Oh, Chief," she said, her voice shaking. "Someone was here. They tried to get into the house. Did you see anyone?"

He shook his head. "No. I was on my way back to the station when I decided to swing by and check on you. I was concerned because your lights were out but your car was here."

"Oh, thank you so much. I believe someone cut my power." She held out the pieces of her phone. "I dropped it. I think it's ruined."

The chief took the phone and looked at it. "I think it will be fine, Mrs. Grant. The faceplate fell off, that's all. I can fix it for you later. Right now, I want to check out your house. Why don't you and Jake get in my car while I look around?"

She nodded and called to Jake, but he wasn't having it. He wouldn't budge.

"You might as well let him go with you," she said to the chief. "He's not the kind of dog to sit in the back of a car when he thinks I might be in danger. He's a great tracker. He can show you the path the intruder took outside."

In spite of the seriousness of her situation, the chief smiled. "Okay. You get in car. Jake can come with me."

Looking around to make sure she was safe, Priscilla jogged over to the police cruiser. She opened the passenger side door and slid into the front seat. Then she closed the door and locked it. Maybe that was silly. She was with the chief of police, and he had a gun. Priscilla suddenly realized she was shaking. Why had someone tried to get into her house? They must have known she was alone. Was it the same person who tried to run her off the road? Did they want her dead?

She took two deep breaths and blew them out slowly, trying to calm her nerve-racked body. She'd just finished her second breath when she saw a car driving up the road. Had the intruder come back? But as the car drew near, she realized it was Gerald's black SUV. In all the excitement, she'd forgotten about their date. When he pulled up next to her, she got out of the cruiser and went to meet him.

"What's going on?" he asked when he got out of his car. "Are you all right?"

"I'm fine," Priscilla said. "Someone tried to break in, Gerald. I think they shut off my electricity." As soon as she said the words, the lights suddenly blazed on. A few seconds later, the chief walked around the side of the house. When he saw Priscilla and Gerald, he joined them. Jake followed behind him as if he were part of the chief's team.

"Hello, Gerald," the chief said when he saw him. "Glad you're here."

"Me too," Gerald said. "What's going on?"

"Not sure, but it seems as if someone was trying to break into Mrs. Grant's house." He turned to look at Priscilla. "He turned off your lights at the fuse box. You might think about getting that moved inside one of these days. A lot of older houses have their fuse boxes outside, but it's a good idea to have them relocated. I think you can see why."

"Chief, I'm really worried about this," Gerald said. "First the incident on the road. Now this."

"That's exactly why we've been keeping an eye on Mrs. Grant. I'd just come by to check on her when I saw the lights out."

"Did you pass anyone on the road, Chief?" Priscilla asked.

"Not on the road that leads to your place," he said, "but there were a couple of cars coming from this direction on the main road. I didn't pay attention to them, I'm afraid. Lots of residents use that road." He fixed his gaze on Priscilla. "Mrs. Grant, has there been anyone hanging around who made you uncomfortable? Someone new in the area?"

Priscilla thought for a moment. "No, I don't think so…" Suddenly, a thought jumped into her mind. "Wait a minute."

"Yes?" the chief said. "Tell me. No matter how insignificant it seems now."

"There's a guy. His name is Tucker...Tucker..." She sighed with exasperation. "I can't remember his last name."

"Tell me about him," the chief said.

"He showed up on Tuesday, I think. Wanted to sketch the cottage and the lighthouse. But that happens a lot, Chief. I'm used to it. Nice guy. I can't believe he'd be involved in this."

"Let me be the judge of that," the chief said. "I really need you to remember his last name if you can."

Priscilla racked her brain, trying to remember, but she just couldn't. "I'm sorry, Chief. My mind is so rattled right now, I can't think clearly."

"Don't worry about it," he said gently. "If you remember, call me right away, okay?"

"I will."

"So now what?" Gerald asked the chief.

"Looks like you two were going somewhere?"

Priscilla nodded. "We were going out for supper."

"Why don't you go on? I'm going to keep looking around. Some of my people are coming out. We'll be looking for fingerprints and other evidence."

"Should you have touched the fuse box?" Gerald asked.

The chief took a handkerchief out of his pocket. "I was careful not to disturb any prints, but to be honest, the switches are pretty small. I doubt we'll get any solid prints from there. All we can do is try."

"Let's go to dinner," Gerald said to Priscilla. "Let the chief do what he needs to do."

"How long will you be here?" Priscilla asked.

"At least a couple of hours. I won't leave before you come back."

"Okay," she said to Gerald. "Can we take Jake with us?"

"Why don't you leave him with me?" the chief said. "We're getting along pretty well."

Priscilla reached down to pet Jake's head. "Sometimes he runs off."

"Does he have a leash?"

She nodded. "But you don't want to mess with him while you're working."

"Why don't you let Jake and me worry about that."

It was clear to Priscilla that the chief was trying to give her some time to unwind. Jake didn't run off as much as he used to, and he seemed pretty intrigued by the chief. "Okay. I'll go inside and get his leash."

The chief shook his head. "I'd rather you didn't go back in just yet. Can you tell me where his leash is?"

"I—I guess so, but I also need my purse and my coat."

"Not a problem," the chief said. "Just tell me where everything is."

Priscilla told him where Jake's leash was, as well as her coat, which she'd already gotten out and put over the back of the couch. "My purse is on the couch, next to my coat," she said.

"Okay. Stay here. I'll be right back."

As he walked away, Priscilla said, "Why can't I go in my house? The intruder didn't get inside."

"I suspect it's because the chief isn't sure about that."

"But I am."

Gerald eyebrows shot up. "Really? How can you be absolutely certain?"

As she thought about it, Priscilla realized the intruder could have headed to the side door while she was focusing on the front door. She hadn't considered that. The thought frightened her. "I—I guess I'm not completely sure."

"Then let's allow the chief to do what he feels he should while we get something to eat. You must be hungry."

Priscilla hadn't even thought about food since the lights went out. But now that Gerald brought it up, she could feel her stomach clamoring to be fed. "I guess I am." She smiled at him. "Let's go."

They waited until the chief brought Priscilla's coat and purse. While Gerald helped her with her coat, Chief Westin attached Jake's leash to his collar. Jake smiled sloppily at the three of them. This was an adventure, and he was definitely excited about it.

After saying goodbye to the chief and rubbing Jake's head, Priscilla walked over to Gerald's SUV and got in. As she waited for him to start the car, she stared at the cottage. The lights from the chief's cruiser flashed, creating a dazzling exhibit of dancing red and blue lights. In the distance she could hear sirens. Within seconds, three other police cars pulled up, adding to the dreadful light show. As the officers got out and met the chief at the front of her cottage, Priscilla began to wonder if life would ever get back to normal.

CHAPTER THIRTY-TWO

When he asked where she wanted to eat, Priscilla picked the Inn even though she was supposed to meet her cousins there tomorrow. She wanted to tell Tilly about Dora. Once that was done, they could choose a different restaurant for lunch tomorrow. After they'd been seated, Hilda came up to the table. She certainly seemed a lot happier since the last time Priscilla had seen her. Her eyes sparkled, and her wide smile made it clear that circumstances must have changed in her life.

"How's your husband, Hilda?" Priscilla asked.

She grinned. "He got a job. Joe Carter, you know, the guy who owns Carter's Hardware store in Vineyard Haven? He actually called Leon because he heard Leon was looking for work. Joe's kids were helping him, but they've gotten pretty busy with their own lives. Joe hired Leon to help him out. Leon loves it." She shook her head. "And a couple of local churches contacted us. Gave us some food and financial help. I don't know how they found out we were in trouble, but Joe was out of work a month. With the assistance we received, we were able to completely recover from the loss of a paycheck during that time. God is good, isn't He?"

"Yes, He is," Priscilla said. She was sure Trudy had opened that door for Leon, and she knew that Trudy's church and her own church had reached out to help them. But she had no intention of telling Hilda that. She and Trudy were big believers in not letting your left hand know what your right hand was doing. "I'm so happy to hear this good news," she said. "Congratulations."

"Thank you." She flipped her order pad open. "What can I get you to drink?"

Priscilla sighed. "I want coffee, but I've had too much lately. I think if I cut myself, I'd bleed caffeine."

"We have a great decaf," Hilda said. "You can't tell the difference between it and our regular coffee."

Priscilla had never found a decaf she liked, but it wouldn't hurt to try one more time. It would be nice to enjoy a cup of coffee without the side effects.

"I'll give it a shot if you will," Gerald said.

"Sounds good. Two cups of decaf, Hilda," Priscilla said with a smile.

As Hilda hurried away, Gerald leaned in close. "So which cousin recommended Leon to Joe Carter?" he asked in a low voice so no one would overhear.

Priscilla grinned at him. "Trudy. But don't tell Hilda or Leon. She wouldn't want them to know."

"I won't, but I think it's terrific."

"I do too. Hilda and Leon are such giving people. They're always helping others in need. I'm glad that when they needed assistance, it was available."

A few minutes later, Hilda returned with their coffee. Gerald and Priscilla both ordered the special—glazed salmon with wild rice.

"So do you think the guy who's been drawing the lighthouse is the same one who tried breaking in tonight?" Gerald asked after Hilda walked away.

Priscilla sighed. "I don't know. He seemed so nice. I never even considered him, and I was actually looking for someone new in the area. He just never occurred to me."

"I'm not an expert on evil stalkers," Gerald said, "but my guess is they try hard not to seem suspicious.

"I know that. But... Well, my alarm didn't go off."

Gerald laughed. "Your alarm? You have an alarm?"

Priscilla nodded. "I have a pretty good sense of people. Sometimes, for no obvious reason, I get bad vibes about certain people. It doesn't work all the time. But this time it didn't work at all."

"Hopefully, Chief Westin will find him. But for now, let's just enjoy our evening."

"And ignore all the evil stalkers?" Priscilla said with a smile.

"Yes. I want to enjoy my salmon. How about you?"

Priscilla frowned at him. "Salmon..." she said slowly.

"Is something wrong?" Gerald asked.

"No, not really. I've been trying so hard to remember Tucker's last name. Then you said *salmon*."

"You think this guy's name is Tucker Salmon? I'm not sure, but it seems to me there's a joke in there somewhere."

"Tucker Salmon," Priscilla said softly. "Tucker Salmon. Tucker..." She suddenly snapped her fingers. "I've got it!" She started to reach for her phone when she remembered it was back at the house. "Gerald, I need to borrow your phone. Please. It's an emergency."

Gerald reached into his pocket and handed his phone to Priscilla. "Hey, Chief," she said when he answered. "I just remembered Tucker's last name. It's Samuels. Tucker Samuels."

She listened for a moment. Then she smiled. "You're welcome." She hung up the phone and handed it back to Gerald.

He looked at her with amusement. "So salmon reminded you of Samuels?" He chuckled. "Good thing we didn't order the rib eye."

"You're right. I don't think that would have helped me at all." She grinned at Gerald. Priscilla really did enjoy spending time with him. She always felt better after being around him for a while.

"I have something to tell you," he said.

Immediately, Priscilla's stomach tensed. This was it. He was leaving. He'd asked her to dinner to give her the bad news. She didn't say anything, just stared down at the table, praying she wouldn't cry.

"Nick turned down the job," he said.

It took a few seconds for Priscilla to understand what he'd just said. "So...so you're not leaving?"

"No. I'm afraid you're stuck with me for a while."

Priscilla nodded and picked up her coffee cup. She needed to do something with her hands. They shook slightly as she raised the cup to her lips.

"You could say something," Gerald said. He was watching her, and it made Priscilla nervous. She didn't want him to see how relieved she was.

She put down her cup and managed a smile. "I'm sorry Nick didn't get the job," she said, "but I'm glad you're staying here. I'd miss you if you left."

"I'd miss you too," he said. "You know, I think we need to talk about..."

The words died on his lips as Tilly suddenly appeared at the table.

"Good evening," she said with a smile. "So glad you're back." She sat down in the empty chair next to Priscilla. "I heard Charles turned up," she said softly. "Did he have the painting?"

Priscilla shook her head. "No. It looks like Charles took off for...other reasons."

"Because of the trouble he got into a couple of years ago?" Tilly asked. When Priscilla didn't respond, she said, "I know all about it. I visited him a few times while he was in rehab. He took his situation seriously, and I've never known him to be dishonest."

"The chief still has to consider him a suspect, but right now it doesn't look like he's our guy." She cleared her throat. "Uh, you probably should also know...Billy didn't take the Adair from the exhibit. Raymond did."

Tilly's eyes widened, and her mouth dropped open. "What? Are you sure? How do you know? Do the police know? Did your mother know?"

Priscilla laughed. "I tell you what. Very soon you and I and the others will get together, and I'll tell you everything I learned today."

Tilly sighed. "It's hard to imagine that anyone in the collective was involved in stealing that painting. When we first started meeting, we were all pretty close. You know, Raymond was really nice. Funny. Kind of the class clown. But you know, he changed later. I'm not sure why, but we suspected it was because of his gambling problem. He got in pretty deep. We never talked about it, and we never thought of that as a motive for stealing. Maybe that's why he took the Adair...if he did."

"Hopefully, the chief and the FBI will get it all figured out," Priscilla said. "I certainly would like to know where that painting is. I hope it isn't destroyed before the authorities can recover it. It's really gorgeous."

Tilly nodded. "Yes, it is. I love my print, but I'm sure the original is even more breathtaking." She shook her head. "I wonder if we'll ever really know all the details. I hope the truth didn't die with Raymond."

Priscilla smiled. "Actually, I've been able to uncover quite a bit about what happened around the time the Adair was stolen."

"How did you do that?" Tilly asked.

"I met Dora Metcalf."

Tilly's perfectly drawn eyebrows shot up. "Dora? You spoke to her?"

"Yes. Mildred was right. She's living with her daughter in Vineyard Haven. She asked me to contact her friends and let them know. That's why we're here."

Tilly's eyes grew shiny, and she blinked back unshed tears. "If she wants to see me, I'd really like to visit. Can you give me her contact information?"

Priscilla nodded and leaned over to get her purse. She took out her notepad and copied Dora's address and phone number on a blank sheet of paper. She tore it out and handed it to Tilly.

"Thank you so much," Tilly said, her voice husky. "I'll contact her tomorrow. I can hardly wait to see her again." She leaned back in her chair and sighed. "The events this week certainly have brought the past back. My emotions are up and down. I'm happy to hear that Dora wants to see me. But I'm sad for everyone involved, especially Skippy."

"What did you say?" Priscilla almost dropped her coffee cup.

"I said I was sad for..."

"You said *Skippy.*"

Tilly's eyes widened. "Did I? How odd. It just slipped out." She laughed. "When the collective first started, we adopted a nickname for Raymond. Because he ate peanut butter every day. I mean... *every* day. We dropped the nickname later when Raymond asked us to. He didn't like being called Skippy, I guess." She smiled. "Understandable. Funny, I'd forgotten all about it."

Priscilla reached out her hand. "Gerald, give me your phone again, please. I know who stole *Seascape in Shadows.*"

CHAPTER THIRTY-THREE

Adrian opened the door a few seconds after Priscilla knocked. "Charlotte," he said with a wide smile. "How nice of you to come by. It's a little late, isn't it?"

"I'm sorry, Adrian," she said. "I need to talk to you. Can we come in?"

Adrian looked past her to see Gerald and Chief Westin standing there. "Of course. Who are your friends?" He swung his door open and Priscilla walked past him, Gerald and the chief following behind. At least Adrian didn't think they were other members of the collective.

"This is Gerald O'Bannon, my friend," Priscilla said, gesturing toward the two men. "And this is Chief Westin from the police department."

"Oh, my. I'm not under arrest, I hope," Adrian said with a smile.

"No, sir, you're not," the chief said. "But we're wondering where your friend Skippy is. We'd like to talk to him."

Adrian shook his head. "I haven't seen him this evening." He frowned. "I'm not sure he'll be back."

"What do you mean, Adrian?" Priscilla said. "Did he tell you that?"

"You know, when he first got here, all he did was talk about a painting. One that went missing years ago. I told him I didn't know anything about it, but I don't think he believed me. Then a few days ago he finally quit talking about it. I was relieved, but he wasn't as nice to me after that. I felt like he was just biding his time. Waiting for...something." He pointed his finger at Priscilla. "I hate to think he was involved in something dishonest, Charlotte, but I just don't trust him."

Priscilla thought for a moment. She needed to make sure of something, but she didn't want to upset Adrian or make her question seem odd. Finally, she said, "Adrian, do you remember why we started calling Raymond *Skippy*?"

He looked at her as if she were simple. "Of course I do. I'm not feebleminded, you know. It was because of all the peanut butter he ate." He shook his head. "He doesn't seem as attracted to it now though. Maybe he got tired of it."

Priscilla turned to the chief. "Can I speak to you outside for a moment?" When he nodded, Priscilla smiled at Adrian. "We're going out in the hall for a few minutes. We'll be right back."

"All right." Adrian stared at Priscilla for a moment. "Is Skippy in trouble?"

"I'm not sure, Adrian," she said. "But he might be."

"Oh, dear. I hope it isn't because of something I did."

"Of course not," Gerald said. He directed his attention to Priscilla and the chief. "You two go on. I'll stay here with Adrian."

Priscilla led the chief to Adrian's door. She opened it, and as soon as they were on the other side, closed the door behind them.

"Adrian thinks I'm my mother," she told the chief. "He thought Joan was Alma Whitaker. It's obvious he thinks his aide, Preston, is Raymond Hill. I haven't seen a picture of him, but I'm betting they look a lot alike. I think it's possible Preston is Raymond Hill's son. And I believe he came here trying to find the Adair. He had the copy that his father stole from Billy and brought it with him. It looks like not long after Preston arrived in town fate stepped in. The painting showed up. Then Preston—or whatever his name is—decided to take it."

"But why hang around? Why didn't he take off once he had the painting?"

Priscilla shrugged. "You'll have to ask him, but I wonder if our visit had something to do with it. If he disappeared right after we came by, wouldn't it look suspicious?"

"Maybe, but to be honest, Adrian Deering wasn't even on my radar."

"But Preston didn't know that. Besides, it wasn't hard to imagine that eventually I'd tell you about Adrian—and Preston. If you looked too closely at Preston Smith you might have discovered he wasn't who he claimed to be."

Someone called out the chief's name. Special Agents Baxter and Peel came walking down the hall. "Thanks for calling us, Chief," Agent Baxter said. "You think you might know who took the painting?"

"Maybe," he said.

As the chief explained everything to the agents, Priscilla went back into Adrian's apartment. Adrian and Gerald were deep in conversation.

Gerald looked up when Priscilla came in. "We'd better get going," she said.

He stood up and extended his hand to Adrian. "I'm so glad I got to meet you," he said. "I hope you'll allow me to come back sometime."

Adrian smiled. "I would like that. Thank you, Gerald. I'm glad you and Charlotte are friends."

"I am too. I'll see you soon."

Priscilla said goodbye to Adrian and followed Gerald out into the hallway. Gerald closed the apartment door behind him.

"I don't think he knows anything about the painting," Gerald said softly. "He remembers the collective and the people who were part of it, but when I asked him about the painting, although he knew it was stolen, he didn't connect it to anyone in the group."

"I think you're right," Priscilla said. "But the members of the collective all suggested that Adrian knew something. That's probably why Preston, or whatever his name is, came here."

"Any idea why he took off now?" Gerald asked. "Something must have spooked him."

"I don't know," Priscilla said. "I just hope the authorities find him before he disappears forever with that wonderful painting."

"Priscilla, this guy tried to hurt you twice," Gerald said, his face tight with concern. "Why? You must know something. Something that could hurt him."

Priscilla held her hands up. "I can't think of a thing. I don't know what he thinks I know. It's driving me nuts."

Gerald smiled. "Well, don't go nuts. Let's see if the chief needs us. If not, let's go back to the Inn and get some dessert. I didn't get to finish my dinner, and I'm still hungry."

"Okay." Priscilla was still a little hungry too, and she wasn't ready for the night to end. They found the chief still talking to the FBI.

"Special Agents Baxter and Peel are going to talk to Adrian," the chief said. "And I'm going to put out a BOLO for this Preston guy."

"You have his real name, Chief?" Priscilla asked.

The chief nodded. "It's back at the station, in the research info we got on Raymond Hill. Can't quite remember it, but I think it's Peter Hill."

"We'll walk you out, Chief," Gerald said.

The three made their way out of the nursing home. When they reached the outside, Gerald asked the chief to wait for a moment.

"I'm concerned about Priscilla going home," he said. "She shouldn't be alone until you find this guy. For some reason, he seems intent on hurting her."

The chief nodded. "I agree. Until he's in custody, you need to stay with someone," he said to Priscilla. "My guys are done at your place, but I'm going to call Teddy and ask him to meet you there. Get some clothes and your dog. Move in with one of your cousins until we can be absolutely certain you're safe."

Priscilla wanted to argue with the chief, but she couldn't. He was right. If only she could figure out why Preston or Peter felt she was such a threat to him.

A van belonging to the nursing home pulled up next to them and parked. One of the staff members got out and smiled at them. He walked around to the large door on the side of the van and slid it open. Several elderly people got out, one by one, helped down from the van by the attendant who had driven them.

"Bingo night," the attendant said to them with a smile.

Priscilla noticed that the residents looked happy. It was great that the home provided trips out. Being stuck inside all the time would drive Priscilla up the wall.

As the residents headed for the entrance, something struck her. She walked away from Gerald and the chief and went around to the back of the white van. It only took a couple of seconds for her to see what she expected to see.

"I think I know why Peter has been trying to silence me," Priscilla said. "At least this last time."

Gerald and Chief Westin came back to where she stood, pointing at the van's window where someone had placed a decal with the home's name on it.

"It was a van just like this one that tried to force me off the cliff," she said.

"And it passed me on the road tonight when I was on my way to your house," the chief said grimly.

"This is what Peter was afraid of," Priscilla said. "That I'd recognize the van and tie him to the attempt on my life."

"I think you're right," the chief said. "Now all we have to do is catch this guy."

CHAPTER THIRTY-FOUR

Priscilla woke up when she heard Joan's phone ring. She rolled over and looked at the clock near the bed. Seven o'clock. She smiled. Gail still called Joan every morning. It was a habit they'd started years ago. Priscilla wasn't sure why, but she suspected Gail wanted to make sure Joan was up in time for work. At one time, Joan seemed to have a problem with being late. Although she'd improved, it appeared the cousins had decided they liked starting the day with each other. It was sweet.

Priscilla rolled onto her back. She tried stretching, but Jake was lying across the bottom of the bed. At first, Joan wasn't too thrilled about Jake sleeping on the bed, but she gave up after he made it clear he had no plans to be separated from his mistress. Dogs seemed to know when their human friends needed protection, and trying to talk them out of it was useless.

Joan's guest room was really comfortable. The mattress on the bed was softer than Priscilla's. Although it might not be the best for her posture, it gave her an incredible night's sleep. She lay there for a while, not really wanting to get up but knowing she should. She and Joan had talked till nearly midnight, with Priscilla filling her cousin in on the latest art heist news. Finally, she swung her legs over the side of the bed and sat up. Jake grunted. It seemed he'd slept pretty well too.

"We probably need to get up," she told him, rubbing his soft head. "Thanks for staying by my side. You're a blessing, Jake."

He sat up and stared at her. Some people say dogs don't smile, but Priscilla was convinced they were wrong. Jake's mouth was curled up in what couldn't be anything but a doggy grin. She reached over and gave him a hug. Then she got up and grabbed her robe. It took her a while to find her makeup case, but when she did, she found her brush and used it to tame her bedhead. Once she finished, she headed for the bedroom door. "Are you coming?" she asked. Jake responded by jumping down from the bed and running over to her side.

Priscilla went into the kitchen where Joan sat at her kitchen table, drinking a cup of coffee. "There you are," Joan said. "How did you sleep?"

"Lying down," Priscilla replied. It was an old joke between her and Rachel. Thinking about her daughter made Priscilla realize she was going to have to call her. Frankly, she'd hoped whoever had been targeting her would be in jail before she had to tell Rachel all that had been happening. But maybe that wasn't going to happen. Rachel would be angry enough that Priscilla had waited this long.

"You're very funny," Joan said with a smile. "Let me reframe my question. Did you sleep well?"

"I did," Priscilla said, sitting down in a chair at the table. "That might be the most comfortable mattress in the known world."

Joan laughed. "I think you're exaggerating, but it is comfy. I wanted something guests would enjoy."

"I may have to move in permanently."

"You'd be more than welcome." Joan stood up. "How about some breakfast?"

"Don't you need to get to work?"

Joan shook her head. "Not today. I'd already planned to take it off. Believe it or not, they still owe me more time. We were so shorthanded during the flu season, and I worked a lot of overtime. This season was the worst I can remember."

"So I heard," Priscilla said. "I'm so glad I didn't get it."

"Me too." Joan went over to the oven and took out a pan.

Priscilla sniffed the air. "Don't tell me..."

Joan grinned at her. "Bread pudding and coffee."

Forty years ago, Joan won a baking contest with her recipe for bread pudding. It was so good several of the restaurants in town served it. It was an incredible dish with cinnamon, brown sugar, and a warm vanilla sauce that seeped down into the bread, making it soft, gooey, and delectable. Priscilla's mouth began to water.

"You are too good to me," she said. "Now I really won't want to leave."

Joan snorted. "I don't make this every day, you know. Most breakfasts are a quick granola bar and a fast cup of coffee."

"Well in that case, I'll go home."

Both women laughed. Joan got out some plates, cut the bread pudding into slices, and poured the vanilla sauce from a pan on the stove over the warm bread. She handed Priscilla a plate, got her a fork, and then poured her a cup of coffee. Priscilla was just taking her first bite when the doorbell rang.

"I don't care who it is," Priscilla said, talking around a mouthful of Joan's delicious creation. "Tell them to go away."

"Oh, hush and eat your breakfast."

Joan left the room to answer the door. Priscilla couldn't see her, but she could hear her talking to someone. She'd just taken a second bite when Chief Westin walked into the kitchen. Priscilla tightened her robe, feeling uncomfortable greeting the chief of police in her nightclothes.

"I'm sorry, Chief," she said. "I just got up." She glanced down at her robe. At least she was dressed modestly.

"Please don't worry about it," he said with a smile. "I've seen women in robes before. My wife even has one."

Priscilla laughed as Joan invited the chief to sit down. "How about some bread pudding and a cup of coffee?" she asked him.

Although at first it looked like he would turn her down, he glanced over at Priscilla's plate. His face showed a brief struggle. The side that wanted to say no obviously lost. "Well, maybe just a small piece," he said, sitting down across from Priscilla.

Jake went over and put his head on the chief's leg. "Well, hello there, Jake," he said gently as he stroked Jake's head. "I'm glad to see you again."

"Looks like you made a real friend there," Priscilla said.

Joan gave the chief a piece of bread pudding, cut one for herself, and then poured another cup of coffee for him. Priscilla noticed that Joan had ignored the chief's request for a small serving. She must have realized that he only said it to be polite. His smile showed his relief that Joan had given him a bigger piece.

Priscilla waited until he'd taken a bite before saying, "What can we do for you today, Chief?"

The chief put his fork down. "I just thought you'd want to know that Peter Hill is in custody."

Priscilla's mouth dropped open in surprise. "You got him? What about the painting? Did you find it? Is it okay?"

Chief Westin laughed. "Slow down. Let me take each of those questions one at a time. First of all, I didn't get him. The FBI did."

"How?" Joan asked.

The chief took another bite, chewed it, and swallowed. Then he washed it down with a swig of coffee. "Fifty years ago, Raymond Hill had someone set to buy *Seascape in Shadows* for five hundred thousand dollars. His son figured that if he could get that much back then, surely it would be worth a lot more now."

"How much is it worth, Chief?" Joan asked.

"I'm told it's valued at a little over a million now."

Joan whistled. "Wow. So Priscilla had a million dollars hanging over her fireplace."

"That's just scary," Priscilla said.

"Well, it seems that Hill Junior didn't have the skills of Hill Senior. Although he's lived his life working with criminal elements, which is the reason we couldn't locate him, he'd never tried to sell a valuable painting. The first person he contacted backed out. But that guy referred him to someone else who told him to stay in Tisbury. He'd come here to pick up the painting."

"Is that why he didn't leave right away?" Priscilla asked.

The chief nodded. "He wasn't happy about staying. He told the man who wanted the painting that he had to meet him last night—or he'd leave with the painting. He said things were too hot here."

"So did the guy meet with him?" Joan asked.

"Yes and no. Someone met with him, but..."

"It was a sting!" Priscilla said.

The chief smiled. "Yeah. The man he met with was Agent Baxter posing as a middle man who handled fine art transactions. The FBI contacted Baxter and Peel and set up the sting. Hill was arrested on the spot. He's sitting in my jail until the feds can arrange for a transfer."

Priscilla breathed a big sigh of relief. "But why—"

"Let me answer your other questions before you hit me with new ones," the chief said. "We have the painting. It's fine. The paint from your picture hasn't been removed yet. The painting is being sent to Boston to be restored."

"What will happen to the fake painting?" Priscilla asked.

"It will be kept as evidence for now. After that, authorities will try to return it to its owner—or the closest relative."

"If they can't find anyone?" she asked.

"It will probably be auctioned off with unclaimed property." He stared at Priscilla over the rim of his coffee cup. "I take it you'd like it if it becomes available?"

"I-I'd like to see it go to Tilly Snyder. She loves that painting."

"I can't promise anything, but I'll do my best," the chief said.

"So has Peter confessed to everything?" Priscilla asked.

The chief grunted. "He's singing like a bird. The feds offered him a deal. Seems he's had business relationships with some very unsavory people. For turning on them, they're offering him a reduced sentence. He'll still do prison time, but not as much."

"But what about all the times he tried to hurt Priscilla?" Joan said. "Surely he won't get away with that."

"No. He'll do time for what he did." He sighed. "But attempting to hurt someone isn't actually hurting them. I'm afraid it won't be as much time as I'd like."

Priscilla didn't say anything. She was disappointed to hear that Peter wouldn't pay a higher price, but at least it was over. She could go back to her normal life.

"I get why he wanted to frame me with the painting," Priscilla said. "But why did he try to force me off the cliff?"

"Now that's very interesting," the chief said. "I'll be happy to tell you… for a price."

Priscilla stared at him for a moment. "What kind of price?"

He winked at her. "Another piece of that incredible bread pudding."

CHAPTER THIRTY-FIVE

After giving the chief his second piece of bread pudding, Priscilla and Joan waited for the rest of the story he had to tell them.

"First of all," he said after another bite, "your reputation precedes you, Mrs. Grant."

"What do you mean?" she asked.

"It seems Peter overheard some of the other aides at the nursing home talking about the Adair being found under your painting. The consensus among them was that there weren't any mysteries you couldn't solve. That it wouldn't take long for you to figure out how the Adair found its way there."

Priscilla felt her cheeks grow warm. "That's ridiculous. The police solve crimes. I'm just . . . a puzzle solver."

"Well, regardless," the chief said, "the aides convinced Hill that you were someone to be concerned about. He got the idea of putting the copy of *Seascape in Shadows* in your house so we would be distracted and think you had something to do with it. As far as what happened on the road that night, he was headed to your house with the painting when he realized he was behind you. He didn't think. He just reacted. He thought that if he could get rid of you, it would be safer for him. It didn't take him long to decide it was a mistake.

He *says* he backed off because he really didn't want to hurt you. Then he realized you'd seen his van. He was convinced it wouldn't take you long to find him. When you showed up at the nursing home, at first he thought it was all over. But it was obvious you hadn't connected the van he drove that night to the nursing home. But he was also aware it probably wouldn't take you long to figure it out. He says that last night, before he was scheduled to meet with Special Agent Baxter, he went to your house to threaten you." The chief frowned and shook his head slowly. "I'm not convinced that's true. He was ready to leave town. He thought he had a buyer for the painting. Why would he need to threaten you at that point?"

"What are you saying, Chief?" Priscilla asked.

He cleared his throat and looked down at his plate. "I doubt we'll ever prove it, Mrs. Grant, but the only reason I can think of for him to try to get to you last night...was to silence you. For good. And his claim that he decided not to push you over the cliff on the road that night? I'm not sure I buy it. I think he heard our sirens and ran. I might be wrong, but I believe Peter Hill wanted you dead."

Priscilla could hardly believe her ears. She heard Joan gasp. "Because if I tied the van to the nursing home, it would lead to him."

The chief looked up. "I'm just guessing," he said. "It's possible he was only going to intimidate you the way he had everyone else. But I just have a feeling..." He met her gaze. "Look, I'm probably wrong. Peter Hill has no record of actually killing anyone. Just forget I said anything."

Like she ever could. "I'm just glad he's locked up, and I don't have to worry about him anymore."

"You said he might have been trying to intimidate Priscilla," Joan said. "Who else did he threaten?"

The chief leaned back in his chair. "As Priscilla guessed, he approached Charles Whistler. Told him that if he shared anything about the collective or about his father, he would implicate him in the theft from the police station. He forced Charles to tell him where the painting was being kept."

"He's trying to win back his family," Priscilla said. "Even if Hill couldn't do what he promised, Charles wouldn't want to take chances."

The chief nodded. "That's why he left town. He didn't want to be anywhere near Peter Hill. After Hill found out we had the painting at the station, he set out to blackmail Manny. He threatened his children and his wife. Manny should have come to me, but he was too frightened. Hill found out that during our shift change, everyone gathers in the meeting room. I go over all the information that the previous shift needs to share with the oncoming shift. For about twenty minutes, the only person not in the meeting room is Gabrielle. It was the perfect time for Manny to unlock the back door and lead Hill to the evidence room. It only took him a few minutes to get in, get the painting, and get out."

"Poor Manny," Joan said. "Is he in trouble?"

The chief shrugged. "We're going to do everything in our power to help him and to keep him working at the station. He knows now that if anything like that ever happens again, he's to come and see me immediately. He was just too scared to think."

"Of course, it was Hill who called the station and told you I had the painting," Priscilla said.

"Yes."

"So Priscilla was the only person who could tie him to the theft of the painting, but she didn't know it," Joan said.

"I felt like the answer was right in front of me," Priscilla said. "And it was. I just couldn't remember what the decal on the van looked like. Not until I saw it again."

"Well, the important thing is, we have Peter Hill locked up. He's not going anywhere for a long time, no matter what kind of deal he gets from the Feds."

"And the painting is going back where it belongs," Joan said.

"Eventually," the chief said. "It's a beautiful painting. I'm glad people will get to enjoy it again." He looked back and forth between Priscilla and Joan. "Any other questions?"

"Yes," Priscilla said. "Was Adrian Deering involved with the theft fifty years ago?"

The chief shook his head. "No. He didn't know anything about it. It didn't take Peter long to find that out after he'd spent some time with him. Peter was getting ready to leave Tisbury, deciding there was no way to track down the painting when..."

"I took it in to be cleaned," Priscilla said with a sigh. "If only I hadn't done that."

"Yeah, it's all your fault, Priscilla," Joan said dryly. "If you were a messier person none of this would have happened."

The chief laughed, and Priscilla waved dismissively at her cousin. "Okay, okay. I get it. Not really my fault, but you have to admit it's a bizarre coincidence."

"You're right about that," Joan said with a smile.

"I need to get back to work, ladies," Chief Westin said. "I thank you for the wonderful bread pudding. And Priscilla, if you have any further questions, come and see me. But for now, why don't you relax and enjoy yourself some? You've been through a lot in a very short time."

As he got to his feet, Priscilla stood up too. "I think you're right, Chief. In fact, I feel like throwing a party." She smiled at Joan. "Wanna help me? Let's celebrate by having some people over to my house tonight."

"Not much time to throw something together," Joan said. The edge of her mouth turned up, and her eyes sparkled. "Just the kind of challenge I like. Let's do it!"

"Please, Chief," Priscilla said. "If you get a break this evening, would you stop by my cottage? I owe you so much."

The chief's face flushed. "I arrested you, and you want me to come to your party?"

Priscilla nodded. "You were only doing your job. Thanks to you and Special Agents Baxter and Peel, the mystery is solved, and I'm safe again." She frowned at him. "Are the agents still in town?"

"They are. They will probably head out tomorrow, with Hill."

"Please extend my invitation to them as well." She pointed at Joan. "Party starts at..."

"Seven o'clock," Joan said.

"Sounds good," the chief said. "I'll talk to Peel and Baxter."

"Thanks, Chief." Priscilla walked him to the door and waved goodbye as he drove away. Jake followed her. He seemed sad to see the chief go.

Priscilla went back into the kitchen where Joan had gotten a notebook and a pen. "We better get cracking on these plans," she said. "We need food, drinks, and we need to make some phone calls." She frowned at Priscilla. "You're not the most spontaneous person I've ever met. This is quite a stretch for you."

Priscilla smiled. "The mystery is solved, and Gerald is staying in Tisbury."

Joan laughed. "He is? Now that really is great news. Another reason for celebration?"

Priscilla winked at her. "What do you think?"

"I think we have our work cut out for us, cousin. Let's get busy."

CHAPTER THIRTY-SIX

"Everything turned out great, didn't it?" Joan asked Priscilla as they munched on hors d'oeuvres and a variety of cookies and pastries from Candy Lane.

"Glad Candy could come," Priscilla whispered. "I was going to buy all of this, but when I asked her if she'd like to stop by, she donated it."

Joan laughed. "No wonder she gets invited to all the parties in Tisbury." She looked around. "Where's Gerald?"

"He went to get some punch for both of us." She smiled at her cousin. "Good punch, by the way."

"Nothing difficult. Frozen raspberries, lemonade, and ginger ale."

"Well, it's yummy."

"I still can't believe you fit all these people in here."

"I didn't really," Priscilla said. "Thanks to Trudy bringing folding chairs from her church, quite a few of our guests are sitting out on the patio. The weather finally cooperated."

"Speaking of Trudy, where is she?" Joan asked.

"I'm not sure. I think she was going over to talk to Uncle Hugh." Priscilla looked around the living room. No Trudy. She walked toward the kitchen with Joan behind her. Sure enough,

Trudy, Gail, and Uncle Hugh were sitting at the kitchen table, talking and laughing. Priscilla made her way into the room. "How's it going in here?" she asked.

"Mighty fine," Uncle Hugh said. "'Specially since you've got hummingbird cake."

"I think Candy brought that just for you," Priscilla said. "I'm so glad you're feeling better."

"Pop was pretty sick for a while," Gail said. "He finally started improving a few days ago."

"With all the hummingbird cake he's eaten, I think we can say he's fully recovered," Trudy said, patting Uncle Hugh on the back.

Uncle Hugh grinned at Priscilla. The eyes that looked out from underneath his bushy eyebrows sparkled with humor. He was obviously having a good time.

"Here you are."

Priscilla turned to find Gerald behind her, holding two cups of punch. "You moved. Not fair. I need navigational lights to track you."

"Hello, Captain O'Bannon," Uncle Hugh said. "Didn't know you were here."

"Good to see you, Hugh. I'm glad to hear you're feeling better."

Hugh shook his head and looked at his daughter. "Did you tell everyone in Tisbury that I had the flu?"

"No, Pop. You're a pretty popular fellow, you know. People were worried about you."

"Oh, balderdash." Even though he dismissed Gail's comment, it was obvious it pleased him.

From behind her, Priscilla heard the front doorbell ring. "That's my cue," she said. "I'll be back." She put the cup of punch Gerald had given her on the kitchen counter and headed back to the living room. When she got to the front door, she opened it to find Dora Genner and Cicely standing there. "I'm so glad you could come." She pulled the door open and ushered them in.

"Mom felt pretty good this evening," Cicely said. "She really wanted to accept your invitation. Not sure how long we can stay, but I'm pleased she was able to come."

As they entered the living room, Priscilla scanned the room. Over in the corner, she spotted Tilly talking to Mildred. She held her hand out to Dora. "Can you come with me?" she said. Dora took her hand, and Priscilla led her over to where Tilly and Mildred stood. Even before they reached the two women, Tilly turned and saw Dora. Her eyes grew wide and filled with tears. She took Mildred's arm and pulled her over to where Dora waited.

"Oh, Dora," Tilly said, her voice cracking. "I'm so happy to see you." She put her arms around Dora, who hugged her back.

"I was hoping to see you tonight," Dora said. When she pulled away, Priscilla could see the tears on her cheeks. "Is that you, Mildred?" she said. Priscilla wasn't too sure what Mildred would do, but surprisingly, she seemed very moved.

"Dora," she said. "You're just as pretty as you were fifty years ago."

Dora laughed. "And you're as big a liar as you were fifty years ago."

For a moment, Priscilla wondered if Mildred would get offended, but instead she burst out laughing. Tilly and Dora joined her. For just a moment, Priscilla could see the young women they had once been. Her mother's friends. The thought of her mother overcame her, and Priscilla turned away. Just then the doorbell rang again. Before she could reach the door, Gerald opened it. Charles Whistler came in with his guest, someone he'd offered to pick up from the nursing home. Adrian Deering looked happy to be out and about for a while.

Priscilla went over to meet them. "Hi, Charlotte," Adrian said. "I'm so glad to see you again. Do you know my new friend Charles?" He laughed. "I used to have a student named Charles. A lot younger than this one, but he certainly reminds me of him."

"Yes, I know Charles," Priscilla said. "Can I introduce you to some other friends of mine?"

Adrian nodded. "Sure. I'd be happy to meet any of your friends. I'm glad to see Gerald again."

"It's nice to see you too," Gerald said.

Priscilla steered Charles and Adrian toward the group of women in the corner. She was curious to see what would happen. These women would also be a lot older than the girls he remembered. Would he recognize them?

Tilly spotted them and grabbed Dora's arm. Dora turned and watched Charles and Adrian approach. When Charles reached them, Dora hugged him.

"I'm happy to see you, Charles," she said.

"Me too," he said, his voice low and husky. This had to be quite a reunion. Although he'd seen Tilly and Mildred around town, it was fifty years since he'd last set eyes on Dora.

"Adrian," Priscilla said, "these women are Mildred, Dora, and Tilly. Ladies, this is Adrian Deering."

"Hello, Adrian," Tilly said. "It's nice to meet you."

"You too." He frowned at them. "You ladies certainly look familiar. Do I know you?"

Tilly looked at Priscilla, a question clearly written on her face. Priscilla shrugged. She wasn't sure what to do. As Adrian was talking to Dora, Priscilla leaned close to Tilly and Mildred. "Just take it easy. Don't try to force anything. Let him tell you who he thinks you are. It may take some time."

Tilly nodded. "We'll be careful." She reached out and took Priscilla's hand. "Thank you for this. You have no idea how much this means to all of us."

"You're welcome. I notice Alma didn't come."

Tilly sighed. "Rome wasn't built in a day, and Alma Whitaker won't soften immediately. We'll keep working on her, don't worry."

"Good." Priscilla turned to leave but Tilly pulled her back. "Your mother would be very proud of you," she whispered.

Priscilla felt her eyes grow moist. "Thank you."

She grabbed Gerald's arm. "Let's take a walk, okay?"

"Sure."

Priscilla said hello to Trudy's husband, Dan, who was discussing art with Roxie Darby. Officers Teddy Holmes and April Brown were talking to Joan. They all seemed to be having a good time. Priscilla's eyes drifted to the spot over her fireplace where a new painting would soon hang. Joan had promised that she would paint a rendition of the cottage and the lighthouse. Priscilla knew it would be just as good as the one she lost.

As Priscilla and Gerald reached the front door, the doorbell rang again. Priscilla opened it to find Chief Westin standing there.

"Oh, Chief," she said. "I'm so happy you found the time to come."

"Thanks for inviting me." He looked a little uncomfortable, and Priscilla wondered if she should stay. Then she remembered that Teddy and April were there.

"I'm going out for a bit," she said, "but a couple of your officers are here." She turned and pointed them out. The chief broke out into a wide grin.

"Thanks. I guess I'll go say hi."

"I'll find you when I get back," Priscilla said. She pointed to the table full of food in the living room. "Lots to eat. Help yourself."

"Thanks," he said. "I will."

As they went outside, Gerald and Priscilla said hello to several people sitting out on the patio. Candy's musical laugh floated through the air. It was a great party and a lovely night. Gerald took Priscilla's hand and led her away from the house and over near the cliffs. When they stopped, they looked out on the water. The waves were coming in to the shore, a soft, soothing, almost musical sound. The skies were finally clear, and the moon was full. It was a breathtaking view.

"You certainly pulled this party together quickly," Gerald said. "I'm impressed."

"Not more than I am," Priscilla said laughing. "I couldn't have done it without Joan's help, Candy's pastries, and Trudy's chairs."

"No matter who helped you, it's a very nice party."

"It is, isn't it?"

"I noticed what you did for the members of the Tisbury Collective. That was very thoughtful."

"Dora's daughter told me her mother was ill. I thought it was time for old friends to bury the past and be there for each other."

Gerald nodded and turned his head toward the ocean. "I could stand here all night. Is there anything more peaceful in the entire world than listening to the ocean?"

"I don't know," Priscilla said. "I'd be hard-pressed to think of something better."

Gerald was quiet for a moment. Although he'd let go of her hand when they reached the cliffs, he reached over and took it again. "I didn't want to leave, you know. It was just... Well, right now, I only have Aggie and Ian, and I almost never get to see Ian. If Aggie and the kids moved away..."

"I understand," Priscilla said softly.

Gerald cleared his throat. "I'm not sure you do. I've been wanting to talk to you. To ask you if... Well, if we..."

"What Gerald?" Priscilla said.

He turned toward her and lowered his face to hers. Suddenly, the silence was split with the sound of loud barking. Priscilla turned around to find Jake sprinting for her, Joan running behind him. Jake ran up and jumped up on Priscilla, his paws on her waist.

"I'm so sorry," Joan said as she reached them. She stopped and bent over with her hands on her knees. "He got out before I could stop him. I was afraid he'd run away." She was breathing so fast she could barely get the words out. She held out Jake's leash, and Priscilla grabbed it. Once she had him secured, Gerald reached over and took the leash from her hands. When Joan finally caught her breath, she held out something else to Priscilla. A folder.

"What's this?"

"A drawing. From Tucker Samuels. He wanted to give it to you as a thank-you for allowing him to sketch your lighthouse."

"That's nice," Priscilla said. "He didn't need to do that." She opened the folder and found a beautiful drawing of the lighthouse. She smiled. "It's great, but I know I'll like yours better."

Joan stared at her for a moment. "You have no idea who Tucker Samuels is, do you?"

"Does he have something to do with salmon?" Gerald asked.

Priscilla giggled while Joan looked at him as though he'd lost his mind. "Priscilla," she said, "Tucker Samuels is a well-known artist. This sketch could be worth thousands of dollars."

"Oh, no," Priscilla said firmly. "I'm not going through this again." She handed it back to Joan. "Here, it's yours. The only painting I care about it the one that will come from you."

"I can't take this."

"Either you take it, or I'll throw it in the ocean. I don't ever want artwork from someone famous again. I've had enough."

"All right, I'll take it," Joan said. "But if you ever want it back, it's yours."

Priscilla nodded. "Deal."

"We might as well head back," Gerald said. "Remember what I said about this being the most peaceful place in the world?"

Priscilla smiled and nodded.

"Forget it."

Priscilla laughed and rolled her eyes. She followed Gerald, Jake, and Joan back to the house. Before they were interrupted, she was certain Gerald was going to kiss her. The next time they talked, would she and Gerald finally be able to admit to their feelings? Even though it hadn't happened tonight, she felt in her heart that it would.

Although the last week had been difficult, Priscilla wouldn't want to be anywhere else in the world except where she was right now. She loved her life, and she could hardly wait to see what would come next.

AUTHOR LETTER

Dear Reader,

I hope you're enjoying your visit to Martha's Vineyard. I love writing about this beautiful part of our country. Envisioning majestic cliffs shaped by relentless waves, the sound of the surf, the enchanting songs of seagulls, and the golden beams from historical lighthouses piercing the darkness as they guide ships to safety, thrills my imagination.

Our main character, Priscilla Latham Grant, has inherited property in Martha's Vineyard from her aunt, Marjorie Latham. She's left her farm in Kansas and moved into a lovely cottage near her very own lighthouse. What fun to vicariously experience many exciting adventures and meet a lot of interesting characters as we join Priscilla in her brand-new life in Massachusetts.

Thank you for coming along with us as we sail around Martha's Vineyard!

Happy reading,
Nancy Mehl

ABOUT THE AUTHOR

Nancy Mehl is a best-selling, award-winning author who lives in Missouri with her husband, Norman, and her Puggle, Watson. She's authored thirty books and, in addition to writing for Guideposts' cozy mysteries, is currently writing a new series for Bethany House Publishing. The Kaely Quinn Profiler series will kick off with book one, *Mind Games*, in December of 2018. The last book in her Defenders of Justice Series, *Blind Betrayal*, released spring 2018.

All of Nancy's novels have an added touch—something for your spirit as well as your soul. "I welcome the opportunity to share my faith through my writing," Nancy says. "God is number one in my life. I wouldn't be writing at all if I didn't believe this is what He's called me to do. I hope everyone who reads my books will walk away with the most important message I can give them: God is good, and He loves you more than you can imagine. He has a good plan for your life, and there is nothing you can't overcome with His help."

Readers can learn more about Nancy through her website: NancyMehl.com. She is part of The Suspense Sisters: SuspenseSisters.blogspot.com, along with several other popular suspense authors. She is also very active on Facebook.

AN ARMCHAIR TOUR OF MARTHA'S VINEYARD

Although in my previous book, *Maiden of the Mist*, I wrote about the Fall for the Arts Festival in October on Martha's Vineyard, and I mentioned the festival in *Seascape in Shadows*, there are a host of other events that occur on the island. In fact, there's something going on almost all the time! Keeping with the theme of art, let's talk about the All Island Art Show that takes place in August.

Held on a location called the Campground, in the heart of Oak Bluffs, local artists set up their displays in a large, iconic building known as the Tabernacle. This huge structure has been the site of many religious meetings, as well as other events that showcase Martha's Vineyard and the people who live there. Also on the grounds are the colorful, renowned Gingerbread Cottages. Some of these charming cottages are available to rent for those wanting to experience the exciting happenings held on the Campground throughout the year.

The All Island Art Show is a longstanding tradition that began in 1956. It's a great chance for local artists to share their talent, but it also gives art lovers a chance to take home a piece of Martha's Vineyard. There are also many awards presented during the event, including the coveted Best in Show award.

If you love art, the Martha's Vineyard All Island Art Show is an experience you're sure to enjoy!

SOMETHING DELICIOUS FROM OUR SEASIDE FRIENDS

Priscilla's Special Chicken Salad

Ingredients:

6 cups shredded or diced chicken

½ cup Hellmann's Mayonnaise

4 hard-boiled eggs, chopped

3 Tablespoons sweet pickle relish

1½ cups chopped walnuts

2 cups seedless red grapes, sliced in half

Salt to taste

Directions:

Mix together. Chill in refrigerator for a couple of hours. Spread on bread or croissants.

Read on for a sneak peek of another exciting book
in the Mysteries of Martha's Vineyard series!

Storm Tide
by Elizabeth Penney

Priscilla Latham Grant was halfway to her cousin's house when the first raindrops fell. A gusting wind rattled the November trees, sending a few brown leaves spinning down.

"I hope the storm doesn't get too bad," Priscilla said to Jake, the red and white loveable mutt she'd adopted. He panted in reply. Jake loved riding in the SUV, no matter the weather.

At least it wasn't snow. November in Martha's Vineyard was a time poised between seasons. It could be gloriously warm and golden or frigid and foreboding. "If you don't like the weather, wait a minute," Priscilla muttered. She laughed. *I guess I'm a real islander now.* The phrase was common among New Englanders, and after more than a year on the island, she knew why.

A recent widow, Priscilla had moved from Kansas to the island after her aunt Marjorie unexpectedly left her a lighthouse, complete with a cottage. Even better, her new home included three wonderful cousins her age, a network of Latham relatives, and a rich family history. She was closest to her cousin Joan, and the opportunity to share impromptu meals like tonight was something she treasured.

She drove over a rise lined with venerable maples and spotted the cheerful light of Joan's house twinkling in the rapidly falling dusk. The days were so short this time of year.

"Here we are," she said to Jake. "Ready to see Sister?" A sharp bark and a tail wag greeted her words. Sister was the lively blue heeler mix Joan had adopted in the spring. The two dogs adored each other.

Joan came to the front door to greet them, holding Sister's collar so she wouldn't bolt. "Glad you could come," she called, a wide smile on her elfin features. Petite and trim, Joan wore her dark hair short.

"Thanks for having us." Priscilla went around to the back seat first and grabbed the dish of half-baked roasted potatoes she'd brought as her contribution. They were her signature dish and would finish cooking in Joan's oven. She'd also made a square cake using homemade applesauce from Vineyard apples and a recipe from her mother's vintage cookbook.

One dish under an arm, the other in her hand, she let Jake out of the SUV. He dashed over to Sister, and the pair began their ritual of sniffing noses. Joan shooed them both inside, holding the door for Priscilla to enter.

"Something smells good," Priscilla said. She handed her pans to Joan and pulled off her coat, then kicked off the ubiquitous rubber-soled boots she wore from October to March. The hallway was small and cozy, like the rest of the house. Joan's furnishings and style were simple yet comfortable.

"I made my classic Boston baked beans," Joan said. "They take all day in a low oven." She led the way to the kitchen in the back of the house, followed by two leaping dogs, their nails clicking on the hardwood floors. After she set Priscilla's dishes on the granite counter, she asked, "Would you like tea? I can put the kettle on."

"That sounds perfect. I'm chilled." Priscilla rubbed her hands together with a shiver, noticing the trickles of rain down the picture windows overlooking Joan's garden. Three seasons of the year, the garden featured riotous English-cottage flower beds adorned with trellises and other features. Now the beds were forlorn, only a few bushes with red berries providing interest.

Joan filled the kettle at the sink. "I'll pull the beans out soon, and you can pop in your potatoes to finish up. We're also having spiral ham. I'll warm up slices for us." At the word *ham*, both dogs sat, tongues hanging out. The women laughed.

"Can Sister have a treat?" Priscilla reached into her sweater pocket for the biscuits she kept there for Jake. They weren't ham, but they'd do. At Joan's nod, she gave the dogs each one. Carrying them away in their teeth, both pups plopped under the table with groans.

The women joined them at the table, each holding a mug of fragrant spiced tea. Priscilla took a sip. "I can't wait to see Rachel in a couple of weeks for Thanksgiving." Her daughter, age thirty-three, was a project manager for a telecommunications firm in Kansas City.

"I'll bet." Joan's dark eyes twinkled. "How are things with her and A.J.? Are they still seeing each other?"

"Yes, they are. Although I think the long-distance aspect is wearing on her." A.J. was a tall, handsome, and—most important— kind FBI agent based in Boston. He and Rachel had met on one of her trips to the island.

"I'll bet. It must be hard." Joan's lips twisted in a sympathetic grimace. "Do you think he'll join us for Thanksgiving dinner? He'd be welcome." The Latham cousins were planning a get-to-gether at Joan's sister's house. Trudy had a spacious, hospitable home that could adequately host a large gathering.

"I'm not sure. I'll ask her next time she calls." Priscilla thought about the upcoming holiday. Thanksgiving was one of her favorites, a perfect combination of loved ones and a delicious feast. This thought led to another. "Are you entering the cranberry sauce contest?"

"Of course. The food pantry needs the support, especially at this time of year." Joan picked up a battered cookbook sitting on the table. "I've been browsing this for recipes."

Priscilla reached out a hand. "Let me see." There were more than sauce recipes, but she focused on that section. A recipe featuring blueberries sounded intriguing. "I think I'll get fresh cranberries from Sheila Weller." The Wellers had operated a cranberry bog on the island for decades. Candy Lane Confectionery, a bakery in town, used Sheila's berries for the muffins Priscilla loved. As for the blueberries, Priscilla had frozen some from a local farm.

"That's a great idea," Joan said. "I love visiting Sheila's farm. Much more fun than going to the grocery store."

"I've always wondered how they harvest cranberries," Priscilla said. The tart red fruit didn't grow in Kansas, but it was a major crop in Massachusetts.

"It's interesting, for sure." Joan stirred her tea absently, staring out into the soggy garden. Her eyes widened. "Look at that wind."

As if in response to her words, the gale howled around the eaves of the house with an eerie, rising wail.

Priscilla looked out to see trees bowing in the wind, their branches waving. The tops of small saplings almost touched the ground. "Wow. It's really gotten stronger in the last few minutes."

"Let me check the weather." Joan got up and turned on the weather radio on the counter. The station gave regular forecasts and updates relied upon by coastal residents.

The droning voice conveyed a warning. A nor'easter had strengthened as it turned toward land, and the islands were in its path. Wind gusts over forty miles per hour and downpours were expected. "Travel is not advised," the voice said.

"You might be staying here for the night," Joan said with a laugh. "Let's pray we keep our power."

"I'm happy to stay if I have to." Since her dog was with her, Priscilla didn't absolutely need to go home. As for her property, the hundred-year-old lighthouse had endured many a storm, hurricanes included. What harm could a simple nor'easter do?

A thumping sound drifted into the kitchen. At first Priscilla thought it was a shutter banging against the wall, but then it resolved into fervent knocking.

"Someone's at the door," Joan said. "I can't imagine who."

From her seat, Priscilla could see the visitor when Joan opened the door, the curious dogs at her heels. A drenched young woman dressed in a light coat stood there, shivering. "I think I'm lost," she said. She rubbed her arms, teeth chattering.

"Why don't you come in and warm up?" Joan said. "We should be able to help you find the place you're looking for." Joan helped her take her coat off and showed her in, the dogs eagerly trailing their new friend.

Priscilla stood when they entered the kitchen. She introduced herself, as did Joan.

The young woman reached out a cold, damp hand. "Hi. I'm...Anne. Anne Edwards." She sniffed, then laughed. "Sorry. I think I'm coming down with a cold."

"No wonder." Joan bustled over to the stove to turn on the flame under the kettle. "Have a seat."

Anne pulled out the chair between Joan and Priscilla and sat, moving slowly as though her bones hurt. Jake and Sister vied for pats, and with a laugh, she gave them both a head rub. "They're so cute."

"They are," Priscilla said. "And annoying." Studying the new arrival, she noticed she had pretty, delicate features and almost milky skin. When she bent her head, Priscilla saw she was wearing a wig. Alarm lanced through Priscilla. *Is she ill?* Besides that clue, it was hard to tell, although Anne was very slender and almost frail. The wool sweater and slacks she wore nearly swamped her frame.

Joan placed the basket of teabags in front of Anne. "Pick one." She whirled away to the cupboard and pulled down a mug. "Are you hungry? I can make you a sandwich."

Anne laughed. "My goodness, you're too kind. A cup of tea would be great. I had lunch not too long ago." She checked over the tea selections and chose one.

A minute later, she had her mug of hot water and was dipping the bag. Joan landed in her chair again. "So tell us, where are you headed?"

Anne took a sip before answering. "I'm looking for the Weller Farm. I've rented a cabin there."

Priscilla and Joan exchanged looks. "We were just talking about the Weller Farm," Priscilla said. "The owner sells cranberries. I didn't know she rented cabins."

"Oh yes," Anne said. "She has two or three. They look really cute online."

A retreat to a farm cabin sounded lovely, but at this time of year? Priscilla wondered what was behind Anne's visit to the island. Feeling it would be rude to ask, she refrained from questions. But she couldn't resist commenting, "I hope they're heated. It can get pretty cold out here in November."

"Oh yes. I made sure of that," was the calm reply.

Joan hopped up again and rummaged in a drawer. "I've got a map of the island here somewhere. It's easier to show you than tell you how to get there." She found the map and carried it and a pen back to the table.

Anne scooted closer to watch while Joan drew on the map, giving landmarks as well. "The dirt road to the farm comes up pretty quick," Joan told her. "There is a sign but it can be hard to see, especially when it's dark." Lightning flashed, followed by a thunder crack so loud the house shook. "Or stormy."

"'It was a dark and stormy night...'" Priscilla said, watching the rain sheet down. The rainfall was so dense now, she couldn't see beyond a few feet. Jake whined, pressing his nose into Priscilla's hand. Like many dogs, he didn't like thunder. Sister went deeper under the table.

Their visitor stared out the window. "Wow. It's really getting bad."

"You might have to—" Joan's words were drowned out by another thunderclap.

Lightning danced in the sky, a little too close for comfort, Priscilla thought. "It's right on top of us," she said.

Joan stood and peered outside, her expression worried. Then she went to the back door and opened it to peek out for a better look. "Water is just streaming down the hillside. I've never seen anything like it."

The other two followed and took turns looking outside. Priscilla saw several frothy brown streams winding down through Joan's garden, moving so fast they made little waves when they hit obstacles. "They're tearing up your garden."

Joan's grimace and shrug were illuminated by another flash of lightning. "There isn't much I can do about it."

Thunder resounded again, but this time it was followed by a strange rending sound and enormous thumps and cracks that made their mugs dance on the table. Jake howled, and Sister joined in.

"Guys?" Anne said from her position by the door. "A tree just fell down."

"Let me see." Joan nudged her aside and, heedless of the rain, stepped out onto the deck. "Oh my," she called. "It's one of those big old maples." She stepped back in, brushing the water out of her hair. "It fell across the road." She shuddered. "Thank goodness it didn't fall on my house."

"I'm surprised we—" The lights flickered and went out. "I was going to say, surprised we didn't lose power." Priscilla groaned. "The tree must have taken down the wires."

"This is crazy!" Anne said. "What if I'd been driving under that tree when it fell?"

That was a sobering thought. Priscilla breathed a prayer for all those traveling during the storm. Then she extended her prayers to the whole island. What if trees did fall on people's houses? They could be hurt or killed. Or have to fix their roofs and replace possessions ruined by falling debris or rainwater.

Joan snatched up the receiver to the landline. "Phones are out too." She found her cell and placed a call to the power company to tell them where the outage was. She disconnected with a rueful laugh. "It might be a while. The calls are just pouring in, they said." She studied the screen. "Hope my battery lasts a while."

Priscilla had the same hope regarding her own cell phone. But thinking of more immediate matters, she took a good look around Joan's kitchen, barely able to see anything in the dim, gray light. "I'm glad you have a gas stove. At least we won't go hungry. Though we'd better keep the fridge closed." The rain was slowing for now, but an outage could take hours or even days to fix.

Joan found a candle and lit it. "I can make a fire in the wood-stove to keep us warm. We're pretty much all set." She set the candle on the table. "Can you tell I've been through this before?"

"Totally," Anne said. "In Boston, we don't have this problem too often. But it must be different out here." Then she clamped her lips shut, as though regretting revealing that much.

"It is," Priscilla said. "And to be honest, that's part of the charm." Yes, living on an island sometimes included events that weren't very convenient, like when the boats couldn't run due to weather. But she wouldn't trade her home for anywhere else.

Joan flitted back to the stove and pulled out the bean pot. "These are ready. You'll have to eat with us, Anne. I insist." She turned up the heat and slid the pan of potatoes into the oven, followed by a foil packet of ham.

"That's so kind of you." Anne's smile was wan. "I guess I picked the right house to stop at."

"I'll say." Priscilla injected warmth into her voice, hoping to make the young woman feel welcome. "Joan's doors are always open to stranded travelers."

Blue, red, white, and yellow lights flashed up on the road. Though the early dusk was falling, the strobes pierced the gloom like beacons.

"That was fast," Joan said. "They must have been in the area." She got up from the table again. "The storm has let up a little right now. I'm going out to see what's going on."

"Me too," Priscilla said. She had to admit to being curious about the fallen tree.

In the end, all three of them trudged outside, Anne wearing a borrowed slicker. Joan had told her to keep it for now, since she didn't have anything adequate. They left the disappointed mutts behind, for their own safety. Priscilla saw them watching out the window, the curtain pushed aside and their heads close together.

"Where's your car, Anne?" Joan asked. Priscilla's was the only one in the driveway.

Anne pointed to a small white sedan. "I parked on the road and walked down the driveway. I was afraid I might not be able to turn around."

Priscilla hopped over a stream of water cutting across the gravel. "That was smart. I hope I can get out." The dirt was much softer now and driving on it would only damage the driveway more.

On the main road, a power truck, the town road agent, and a police cruiser were parked near the fallen giant, their lights still flashing. Men in hard hats shouted to each other, and Priscilla heard the distinctive buzz of chain saws.

Priscilla spotted Officer April Brown, the only woman in the crew. "Wild storm, isn't it? I'm so thankful that tree didn't hit Joan's house."

April, watching the work with folded arms, nodded. "Yeah, and this is only the beginning. Another front is moving in." She smiled briefly at Joan and Anne, giving them a small wave. "You were lucky the crew was close by. It's going to be days before we're back to normal." She sounded gloomy.

Priscilla sympathized. April had two teenage boys and a husband at home, but when emergencies arose, she had to work around the clock. It was part of the job.

Judging that it was safe, Priscilla edged closer to the tree. The trunk was massive and gnarled, probably over a hundred years old.

Instead of breaking off, as often happened during a storm, the roots had been torn out of the ground due to the soggy soil.

Priscilla spotted something in the dirt crater created by the roots ripping free. *What is that?* It had a rounded shape and was large. Not a rock, since it was definitely white, not tan or brown or gray.

Seeing that April had moved to the head of the tree, she crept closer. Reaching down, she rubbed mud away, wincing at the stain on her gloves.

Then she yelped. The object had eye sockets. And now that she was closer, she saw stick-like limbs and outstretched finger bones. Something glittered on one phalanx.

She had found a skeleton.

A NOTE FROM THE EDITORS

We hope you enjoyed Mysteries of Martha's Vineyard, published by the Books and Inspirational Media Division of Guideposts, a nonprofit organization that touches millions of lives every day through products and services that inspire, encourage, help you grow in your faith, and celebrate God's love.

Thank you for making a difference with your purchase of this book, which helps fund our many outreach programs to military personnel, prisons, hospitals, nursing homes, and educational institutions.

We also create many useful and uplifting online resources. Visit Guideposts.org to read true stories of hope and inspiration, access OurPrayer network, sign up for free newsletters, download free e-books, join our Facebook community, and follow our stimulating blogs.

To learn about other Guideposts publications, including the best-selling devotional *Daily Guideposts*, go to Guideposts.org/Shop, call (800) 932-2145, or write to Guideposts, PO Box 5815, Harlan, Iowa 51593.

Sign up for the Guideposts Fiction Newsletter

and stay up-to-date on the books you love!

You'll get sneak peeks of new releases, recommendations from other Guideposts readers, and special offers just for you . . .
and it's FREE!

Just go to Guideposts.org/Newsletters today to sign up.

Guideposts.

Visit Guideposts.org/Shop or call (800) 932-2145

Find more inspiring fiction in these best-loved Guideposts series!

Mysteries of Martha's Vineyard

Come to the shores of this quaint and historic island and dig in to a cozy mystery. When a recent widow inherits a lighthouse just off the coast of Massachusetts, she finds exciting adventures, new friends, and renewed hope.

Tearoom Mysteries

Mix one stately Victorian home, a charming lakeside town in Maine, and two adventurous cousins with a passion for tea and hospitality. Add a large scoop of intriguing mystery and sprinkle generously with faith, family, and friends, and you have the recipe for Tearoom Mysteries.

Sugarcreek Amish Mysteries

Be intrigued by the suspense and joyful "aha!" moments in these delightful stories. Each book in the series brings together two women of vastly different backgrounds and traditions, who realize there's much more to the "simple life" than meets the eye.

Mysteries of Silver Peak

Escape to the historic mining town of Silver Peak, Colorado, and discover how one woman's love of antiques helps her solve mysteries buried deep in the town's checkered past.

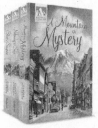

Patchwork Mysteries

Discover that life's little mysteries often have a common thread in a series where every novel contains an intriguing whodunit centered around a quilt located in a beautiful New England town.

To learn more about these books, visit Guideposts.org/Shop